HEAT

BEARPAW RIDGE FIREFIGHTERS BOOK 1

OPHELIA SEXTON

Published by Philtata Press
Text copyright 2016 by Ophelia Sexton. All rights reserved.

Cover Design by Jacqueline Sweet

This ebook is licensed for your personal enjoyment only. This ebook may not be resold or given away to other people. If you would like to share this book with another person, please purchase an additional copy for each recipient. If you're reading this book and did not purchase it, or it was not purchased for your use only, then please return to your favorite ebook retailer and purchase your own copy. Thank you for respecting the hard work of this author.

EXCERPT

The temptation of having Annabeth standing so close to him, surrounding him with her scent, and smiling up at him as her fingers wrapped around his, proved to be too much.

With a low growl, Dane pulled her to him and bent his head. He buried his face against the soft, warm skin on the side of her neck and inhaled deeply.

"You smell so sweet," he whispered and felt her pulse jump against his lips.

Dane took her into his arms, pressing her soft curves against his chest. She fit perfectly against him. She didn't try to pull away. If anything, she leaned into him.

He wanted her with every bone and sinew in his body and with every inch of his soul.

With deep affection and many thanks to Keri and Andy in Salmon, ID for their hospitality and for providing many useful details about ranches and life in a small town. And for not laughing at me for my habit of compulsively locking my car doors while visiting them. It's a tough habit for this urban California girl to break!

Many thanks, also, to KadyG, professional chef extraordinaire, and the ever-imaginative Vinca Minor for helping me brainstorm a Horrible, Awful, No-Good Day for my hapless bakery owner, and to Mike, for sharing his experiences as a volunteer firefighter in a small Idaho town.

1
SHATTERED

Every single delicate cherry blossom intended for Emmaline Chu's wedding cake had been smashed overnight. The crumbled remains of several hundred handmade gum-paste flowers lay scattered across sheets of parchment paper spread over the bakery's stainless steel counter.

The pretty mermaid, fishes, and molded sea shells for Rowan McKenzie's birthday cake had also been destroyed. The mermaid's head stared dolefully up at Annabeth Jones as she stood frozen in horror at the sight.

Annabeth had spent days making those cake decorations, which required at least a day to dry. It was Friday morning, the cakes were due to be delivered tomorrow afternoon, and she didn't know whether to burst into tears or throw up.

It was a disaster.

She would have to spend all day redoing the decorations and hope to God that they dried quickly enough overnight to use. Only then could she get started on baking and frosting the cakes, which had been her main project today.

But Annabeth didn't care if she had to pull an all-nighter. She was *not* going to disappoint a couple on their wedding day. Or a little girl on her birthday.

"Annabeth, what are you…? Oh. My God," said Annabeth's boss Maggie Ornelas as she entered the bakery with her usual energetic step despite the hideously early hour.

She came to a halt next to Annabeth, staring down at the destruction. "What the *hell?*"

Maggie was the owner of Cacao Cakes, a high-end bakery in San Francisco. She had hired Annabeth right out of the culinary institute, and Annabeth had been working for Maggie at Cacao for nearly five years now. Together, Maggie and Annabeth had made Cacao a success, so much so that they were frequently forced to turn away customers who wanted wedding cakes or other special occasion cakes.

"Everything was fine when I left yesterday afternoon," Annabeth said numbly.

She reached out, her hands shaking with shock, and touched the gleaming blue fragment of a shattered fish. She had just finished painting it yesterday with a mixture of lemon extract and pearlescent powdered food coloring.

"And they were fine when I closed at 5:00 p.m.," Maggie said, frowning. "Someone must have done this overnight…let's look at what the security camera caught."

Feeling hollow and shaky, Annabeth followed her boss to the little office in the back of the bakery.

There, she was greeted with her second horrible shock of the morning as they stood in front of Maggie's computer, reviewing the security footage from the previous evening.

"Is that…*Roger?*" Maggie asked with evident disbelief.

Now Annabeth really did feel like throwing up as she saw her fiancé Roger Pemberton calmly strolling in through the bakery's employee entrance.

As both women watched, dumbstruck, he picked up a rolling pin and methodically began to smash each decoration.

Roger had been so angry that Annabeth wouldn't take the day off work yesterday to go furniture shopping with him. She had known he would make her pay for defying his wishes, but she had never, in her wildest dreams, thought he would do something like *this*.

"I'm going to call the police and have them arrest that son of a bitch!" Maggie growled.

"No, please, don't!" Annabeth begged. "I'll fix it, I promise I will!"

Maggie would be within her rights to call the cops, of course, but Roger would blame Annabeth for the humiliation of being arrested.

She shuddered to think how he'd make her pay.

Maggie turned to Annabeth. "How did he get in?"

"I—I fell asleep right after dinner last night. I was really tired," Annabeth replied, unable to tear her gaze away from the monitor and Roger's orgy of destruction. "I guess he took my keys."

Roger had known how hard she had worked on crafting those decorations. She had been telling him about her progress all week. And so, he had decided on the perfect punishment for her…sabotage the work that had kept her from accompanying him to that designer outlet yesterday.

He was the handsomest man Annabeth had ever met, and even now, she couldn't believe that he was actually interested in *her*. That he wanted to marry her.

Her mother had always told her that no man would ever be interested in her until she lost those extra pounds she was carrying.

Roger could be so sweet, so charming. He liked having sex with her, and he often bought her expensive presents. Being with him was good…until she did or said something to make him mad.

And his anger never burned hot. He never hit her or yelled at her. Instead, he would deliberate with icy fury to decide which punishment would hurt her the most, and then he would carry it out.

Last time, it had been her great-grandmother's century-old tea service. Annabeth had forgotten to run an errand for Roger after work. He hadn't said much when she apologized, but after dinner, he had deliberately smashed the fragile bone china cups one by one on the kitchen floor while she wept and pleaded with him.

Then he had ordered her to clean up the mess and walked out of the kitchen to watch television while she swept up the fragments, trying not to sob too loudly, because the sound would annoy him.

"This—this was my fault. I made him angry, and I'm the one who left my keys where he could find them. It won't happen again, I promise. But please don't call the police, Maggie. *Please!*"

"You think that this was *your* fault? Listen to yourself, honey! You need to leave him," Maggie said, shaking her head. "Nothing you do will ever make him happy, and his punishments are going to become more extreme."

"*Leave* him? But we're getting married in a couple of months!" Annabeth protested automatically.

She knew Maggie was right, but she didn't know what she could do.

Roger would never let her leave him.

"Do you have a safe place to go?" Maggie asked, tapping a key and freezing the security footage on an image of Roger, his expression utterly calm as he raised the rolling pin.

"I could stay in San Leandro with Mom for a few days, but after that, I don't know." Annabeth replied, still feeling numb with shock.

"We'll find a solution," Maggie assured her. "You're my best employee. Without all of your hard work and talent, Cacao wouldn't be half the success it is today."

To Annabeth's astonishment, Maggie hugged her, hard. She knew Maggie was angry at what Roger had done. But she should be blaming Annabeth.

"I'll fix everything," Annabeth promised. "And I'll do it off the clock. I feel so bad about this, but those cakes will be ready tomorrow morning if I have to stay all night."

"Nonsense!" Maggie assured her. "Latoya's been asking for more hours. I'll call her to come in this afternoon to do the baking, filling, and frosting, so that you'll have time to redo the decorations." She paused. "I'll make you a deal, Annabeth. If you promise me that you'll go somewhere safe tonight and think about what I said, I won't call the police."

"Okay, I'll go to Mom's place. And thank you," said Annabeth. And then, suddenly, she was crying, great heaving sobs against Maggie's shoulder. "Oh, Maggie, what am I going to do?"

"Look, this is fucking ridiculous," Roger said, sounding impatient over the phone. "You're acting like I *hit* you or something. Come home, Bethie. I promise I'll make it up to you."

Annabeth hated being called "Bethie" by anyone except her mother, but Roger had decided that it would be his special pet name for her, and her protests only annoyed him.

She took a deep breath and tried to keep her voice calm. "Roger, how *could* you do that to me? You knew I had to deliver those cakes this morning! I could have lost my job! And Maggie wanted to have you arrested for breaking and entering. I had to beg her not to do it!"

A long, ominous pause. "Look, I'm really sorry," Roger said at last. "I didn't mean it. Tell Maggie that, okay? But you just made me so fucking angry… Why does your stupid little job always have to come first? Why can't you ever make *me* a priority?"

And just like that, it was all *her* fault. Again.

Annabeth concentrated on breathing and not replying. Whatever she said now, it would only make things worse.

Apology and accusations dispensed with, Roger returned to his most pressing concern. "So when are you coming home? You know I don't like eating dinner by myself or sleeping alone."

"I—" Annabeth bit down on her automatic impulse to apologize. "I need a day. Maybe two."

"A day," Roger countered, his tone implacable. "I want you home tomorrow, Bethie."

"I'll think about it," she said, knowing that she was running the risk of making him angry again.

Would she return to their condo in the hip Hayes Valley neighborhood of San Francisco to find something else she loved either destroyed or donated to Goodwill?

And at that thought, she knew Maggie was right. Things had been getting worse lately. She couldn't go back to him. Couldn't marry him.

The thought of breaking up with him, of telling him that they needed to cancel their wedding plans, made her feel queasy with anxiety. All that money he had already paid in deposits...

"All right," he said coolly. A danger sign. "Love you."

"Love you, too," she said, obediently.

That was one of Roger's rules. She always had to end phone calls, texts, or emails with *I love you.*

"You're not thinking of breaking up with him, are you?" Mom asked anxiously as soon as Annabeth ended the call.

"Yeah, I am. He was really nice when we first started dating, but ever since we moved in together, he's been kind of...abusive," Annabeth said slowly.

"Does he hit you?" Mom demanded, leaning forward to peer at Annabeth's face as if looking for bruises.

"No, but—" Annabeth began.

"People are so quick to use the word *abuse* these days," Mom interrupted, her tone dismissive. "And Bethie, you have to think realistically. He's so handsome, and he's got such a great career going... and then there's *you*." She sighed. "If only you would lose some weight, you'd be a really attractive young woman. But looking the way you do, it's a miracle you managed to snag someone like Roger. You can't count on having the same luck twice."

Annabeth glared at her mother. She'd almost forgotten why she'd been so eager to move out of this house and move in with Roger.

A familiar toxic mix of resentment, frustration, and anger churned in her stomach.

Her phone belted out Maggie's ringtone.

"It's my boss. I have to take this," she said to Mom and walked out of the room to answer her call.

"Hey," she said to Maggie. "I'm at my mom's."

"Good," Maggie said. "I'm glad." She paused. "Um, how did Roger take it?"

"A phone call and five text messages, and he's ordered me to come home tomorrow. He also says he's sorry about what he did," Annabeth said glumly. "Oh, God, Maggie, what am I going to do? I just spent two hours looking at places for rent in the Bay Area, and I can't afford anything within commuting distance of the City. Not even with roommates. Not even with a second job."

Not without using the money in my special savings account. Which she absolutely did not want to do unless it was a dire emergency.

Did breaking up with Roger count as an emergency?

Maggie sighed into the phone. "Well, I may have something for you, but I'm not sure you'll like it."

"At this point, I'm willing to consider *anything*," Annabeth told her.

"Okay, I know I'm shooting myself in the foot telling my best employee this," Maggie said, "but how would you feel about opening your own place, Annabeth? I just finished talking to my big brother Manuel. He's a real estate agent in Bearpaw Ridge in Idaho, and he says that there's a bakery-café in town that needs a new proprietor. I told him that you were a Culinary Institute grad and that you'd worked for me for five years, and you would *not* believe how excited he was!"

"Leave California?" Annabeth asked in disbelief.

And yet, the thought of leaving behind Roger...and Mom...and starting fresh somewhere far away sounded really good right now.

And hadn't she been saving up for years to start her own business?

"You'll love Bearpaw Ridge! I go there all the time to visit my family," Maggie said enthusiastically. "It's a small town, maybe three thousand permanent residents, but it's a really nice place with really friendly people. The kind of place where people don't bother locking their doors…or their cars."

"I don't know," Annabeth said slowly, though her heart was beating with excitement at the prospect. *My own bakery!* But she had to be practical… "Only three thousand people? Is that really enough people to keep a business going? I mean, *why* is that bakery available?"

"The owner retired a couple of months ago and moved to Arizona to be with his grandkids," Maggie said promptly. "He never had any issues making ends meet—there's a lot of tourist traffic, even in the winter, because the town is on the way to that big new ski resort and Bearpaw Springs National Park."

"Well, then, that sounds great, if, uh, kind of far away." Annabeth tried to catch her breath. This was all happening so fast. She really wanted to do it…but could she really pack up everything she owned and move to a place she'd never been?

"So you're interested?" asked Maggie. "Because if you are, I'll tell Manny that you can be there…in a week?"

"A *week?*" Annabeth squeaked. She felt like someone who had just jumped into a raging river and was being swept along in the current.

"You'll want to get yourself up and running as quickly as possible, before Chinook salmon fishing season starts in May and the town is crawling with fishermen looking for hot coffee and a Danish."

I can't, thought Annabeth. *I can't just decide to move to a place I've never even visited, can I?*

"Bethie?" Mom called from the other room. "Roger's on the other line. He wants make sure you're coming home tomorrow. You *are* going home tomorrow, dear? You're not going to do anything stupid?"

Oh yes, I am, Annabeth thought with sudden determination. *I'm about to do something totally stupid and scary.*

"Yes," she told Maggie. "Yes, that sounds really great. Will you email me your brother's info? I'll call him in the morning."

"I'm going to hate to lose you, honey," Maggie said, sounding rueful. "But I'm excited for you, too."

"So am I. Excited and scared," Annabeth said and realized she had made her decision. "Thank you so much, Maggie. You'll come visit me in Idaho, right?"

"You got it," Maggie said. "I can't wait to see how you spread your wings, Annabeth."

Annabeth disconnected, feeling giddy.

Yes, she would go home tomorrow, but she would do it while Roger was at work. She would get her belongings, pack up her car, and head for Bearpaw Ridge.

Everything is going to be different from now on, she told herself. *And I'm going to prove that Mom and Roger were wrong when they told me I could never make it on my own.*

2

FATED

It wasn't even dawn yet, but it had already been a pretty good morning, Dane Swanson thought as he relaxed in the fire engine's cab.

He was bone-tired, and his mouth tasted of smoke and ashes, but that was okay. Dane loved this part of the day, returning to the firehouse when he was balanced on the edge of fatigue and satisfaction.

Dave Zettler's vacation rental cabin was going to need a new roof and a lot of interior work to repair the smoke and water damage, but Dane and his brothers had been able to stop the fire from spreading.

And, most important, the family staying in the cabin had escaped with no major injuries.

"Hey, remember how Manny Ornelas was telling us that he found someone for Frank's place?" Mark asked as he turned the fire engine onto Main Street. "I think they're finally open for business." He sniffed. "And I smell something baking."

Dane's younger brother had won this morning's coin toss as to who got to drive the Bearpaw Ridge Fire Department's big fire engine.

Like Dane—and all the other Swanson brothers, with the exception of Thor, who'd moved to Denver after college—Mark was one of Bearpaw Ridge's volunteer firefighters.

Dane looked ahead and saw that the lights of Frank's Bakery were on, shining like a beacon through the large plate glass windows. All around them, the rest of the town was still deserted and quiet in the gray light of approaching dawn.

"Think they're open? I could really use a cup of coffee and maybe a Danish," Dane's other brother Evan said from the back seat.

"Only one way to find out," Dane said as Mark pulled over and parked the engine in front of the bakery. "And whatever's going on in there, it smells damned good."

A newly painted sign on the glass door read *Cinnamon + Sugar Bakery & Café.*

Underneath, the sign said, *Open 5:00 a.m. – 5:00 p.m., Tuesday – Sunday.*

Both parts of the sign were written in a pink, curlicued font that Dane immediately labeled as "girly."

Not that Dane objected. If anything, Bearpaw Ridge desperately needed more women.

But crusty old Frank Hermann, who was a man's man, would be spinning in his lawn chair if he knew what had become of his bakery.

Dane grinned at the thought as he pushed open the bakery door. It was 4:55 a.m., but the door was already unlocked.

An old-fashioned bell fastened to the inside of the door tinkled as they entered the café area, which had been furnished with new stone-topped tables and chrome chairs in place of the beat-up Formica tables and battered wooden chairs that Frank's establishment had boasted.

Mark and Evan followed close on Dane's heels.

Dane stopped just inside and inhaled deeply as a wave of wonderful smells greeted him like a warm embrace: baking bread, cinnamon, sugar, and vanilla mingled with the scent of freshly brewed coffee.

The display cases near the register were filled with a selection of cookies and miniature fruit tarts, topped with glazed berries and pieces of fruit that gleamed like jewels. There was a tall glass case that held a model wedding cake, which had been beautifully decorated with a lacy pattern of piped frosting and a cascade of lifelike sugar roses.

And then the bakery's new owner hurried from the back.

At the sight of her, curvy and radiant under a turquoise-blue chef's coat decorated with a dusting of flour, Dane suddenly felt like he'd been punched in the chest. He couldn't breathe.

"Hi, I'm Annabeth," she said with a warm smile. "Welcome to Cinnamon + Sugar!"

She paused to look them up and down, and Dane felt another jolt as their eyes met. Hers were dark blue under arched red-gold brows, and a few wisps of curling strawberry blonde hair escaped from under a chef's hat that resembled a beret.

Dane wondered what she saw when she looked at him.

Glancing over at Mark, who looked like a reverse raccoon with his sooty cheeks and wide pale band around his eyes where the goggles had shielded him, Dane could guess that all three of them looked pretty damned funny at the moment.

To her credit, Annabeth didn't stare. Or laugh. Just smiled at them like they were already old friends that she was glad to see.

"You guys just coming back from a call?" Annabeth asked.

Her voice was low and pleasant. Dane felt like he could listen to her all day.

"Uh," he managed. Somehow, he couldn't get his mouth to work properly.

"Yeah," Mark said, grinning at her, his teeth white between soot-stained lips. "I wouldn't be out of bed otherwise. I'm not really a morning person."

She laughed, and Dane felt a sudden, inexplicable stab of jealousy.

"I'm really not a morning person either," she confessed. "But if I'm not up by 2:30 a.m., then I won't have anything ready to sell for breakfast."

Something dinged in the back, and she glanced back over her shoulder.

"And the first pan of cinnamon rolls is ready, and only a few minutes late! If you gentlemen want to help yourself to coffee and take a seat while I put some icing on them, they'll be my treat." She paused, and her smile widened. She added, sounding shy, "Since you're my very first customers and all."

"Thank you, Annabeth," Dane finally managed. "I'm Dane Swanson, and these are my brothers Mark and Evan. And those rolls smell beyond delicious."

She rewarded him with a dazzling smile and vanished into the back of the bakery.

Dane stood rooted to the floor, staring after her, until Evan put a hand on his shoulder and pushed him down into the nearest chair. "Earth to Dane," he said sarcastically. "Come in, Dane."

"Down, boy, and put your tongue back in your mouth," Mark teased him in a low voice.

Annabeth's cinnamon rolls, large enough to fill the entire dessert plate, were *amazing*. Soft and buttery and still steaming hot, with a generous coil of sweet cinnamon filling and topped with a cream cheese and vanilla frosting that had all three Swanson brothers licking their fingers, the treats vanished quickly.

And the coffee was great too. It had been brewed from freshly ground French roast, dark and strong and just what Dane needed to wash the taste of smoke out of his mouth.

Annabeth, who had been bustling between the back of the bakery and the front, filling the display cases with freshly baked and frosted cinnamon rolls, glanced at their empty plates, now decorated with just a crumb or two, and dimpled.

Without a word, she brought the big pan of still-warm rolls to their table.

"These are *amazing*," Dane told her as she lifted her spatula and slid another piece of heaven onto his plate. "You're not going to be able to keep these in stock once word gets out. You'll have people lined up out the door, waiting for them to come out of the oven."

Evan and Mark, their mouths full, nodded enthusiastic agreement.

"Do you really think so?" Annabeth asked, as if she didn't believe him. Her cheeks turned an appealing shade of pink. "I mean, they're just cinnamon rolls, nothing fancy."

"They're *fantastic* cinnamon rolls," Mark assured her, having washed down his mouthful with a swig of the excellent coffee. "And they're going to be a big hit."

"I really hope so," she said. "I've pretty much used up my savings at this point."

Dane looked around at the clean, inviting space. "We'll tell everyone we know to drop by," he promised her. "Just make sure to bake plenty of those rolls."

That won him another smile, and Dane realized he was a goner.

Mark and Evan both snickered at him as soon as Annabeth had bustled off to the back of the bakery again to get the next batch of cinnamon rolls out of the oven.

Dane didn't care. He had just met the woman of his dreams—beautiful, sweet-smelling, kind, and a talented cook.

And, as an added bonus, she had the kind of generous figure that would feel damned good against him when they were both naked in bed. *His* bed.

His inner bear stirred. *Our mate*, it announced.

Dane froze in horror as he realized what his reaction to Annabeth signaled.

There has to be some mistake!

Our mate, repeated his bear with calm confidence.

Dane the man was anything but calm right now. His heart was pounding, and he felt shaky, as if he'd just downed a dozen espresso shots. *It can't be!*

For one thing, underneath the enticing scents of butter, spices, and vanilla, he had sensed that Annabeth was just an Ordinary human.

Not a bear shifter…not *any* kind of shifter. Just an extremely attractive woman.

And for her to become his mate, she would have to learn everything about him. How could an Ordinary human woman ever accept his shifter side?

Dane recalled Tanya's reaction, all those years ago, and winced. That memory still had the ability to sting him with mingled pain and guilt, especially because of what had happened afterwards.

Dane looked over at his brothers, who had finished their second rolls by now and who were eyeing his untouched roll hungrily. With a sigh, he handed it over, and Evan tore it neatly in two, handing half to Mark.

"Let's go," Dane said abruptly. "We still have our morning chores to do at the ranch."

But he found himself unable to leave the premises without one more glance at the delectable Annabeth.

"Thank you!" Dane called and found himself rewarded when she looked up from behind the row of glass display cases she was filling with chocolate-dipped shortbread. She waved at him.

"And good luck," he added, just to see her smile again. "I think you're going to be a big success."

"Hey Annabeth. Can I give you a hand with those?" asked a deep, sexy voice that Annabeth remembered very well.

Annabeth straightened up and instantly wished she'd worn a nicer blouse and put on some makeup to go shopping.

Strolling up the alley behind the bakery was Dane, one of the three hunky firefighters who had made her Grand Opening Day so memorable.

Watching him approach, her heart felt like it was squeezing in her chest.

In the rare quiet moments of her first few days in business, she hadn't been able to stop thinking about the big dark-haired man since he had entered her bakery at oh-dark-thirty in the morning.

Sweaty, exhausted, and smeared with soot, he'd still been the sexiest thing she'd ever laid eyes on, six-foot-three of broad-shouldered animal magnetism with warm hazel eyes under dark brows.

Now, showered and clean-shaven, he was enough to make her want to fling herself at him.

It was 8:00 p.m. on her third day of business, and she had just returned from the long drive to and from the restaurant supply warehouse in Missoula.

When Dane greeted her, she was staring at the huge sacks of flour and sugar piled in the back of her Prius, trying to figure out how to unload her car without giving herself a hernia.

She'd seen a trickle of customers on opening day turn into a flood yesterday, until, as Dane had predicted, she'd had people waiting in line this morning for each fresh pan of cinnamon rolls as they emerged from the oven.

In fact, she'd never even gotten around to making her planned croissants or more than a couple of kinds of cookies yesterday. All the demand had been for her cinnamon rolls, and she'd spent the hours before the bakery opened prepping batches of sweet yeast dough to meet the demand. Each of the pans of rolls sold out within minutes of emerging from the oven.

She was thrilled with the initial success of her venture but had gone through her starter supplies of flour, sugar, and butter with frightening speed. So she had been forced to close the bakery a couple of hours early today and drive up to Missoula to the restaurant supply place.

She had originally planned to keep the bakery open seven days a week, but with the restaurant supply warehouse located over

100 miles away, she quickly realized that she would have to close one day a week to go shopping, if nothing else.

Which led to the problem she faced now...the friendly guys at the restaurant supply company had loaded up her car with several fifty-pound sacks of flour, white sugar, brown sugar, and salt as well as big, plastic-wrapped blocks of unsalted butter, packages of yeast, and baking powder.

Which was great...until she arrived back at Bearpaw Ridge and realized that she was on her own as far as unloading her purchases went.

"You would be my hero if you could help me drag those bags into the storeroom," she said ruefully.

"I'd be happy to," he assured her. "But it's probably easier if you just step aside and let me get them out of there."

*Don't stare. Don't stare. Don't stare...*she repeated fiercely to herself as he bent to grab the first of the bags.

So what if those tight jeans made her want to remove them from that fine, *fine* ass with her teeth?

Bad thoughts, Annabeth. He's just being nice to you because you gave him free food. He's probably married...or gay. All the hunky and nice ones always are.

But watching his muscles move under the tight fabric of his T-shirt as Dane easily hefted all four of the fifty-pound bags out of the trunk of her car only incited more dirty thoughts.

Oh my God, my panties are melting, she thought dizzily, watching him walk to the bakery's back door. *He's incredible...and how the hell is he carrying those bags like they don't weigh a thing?*

"You want me to put these in your storeroom?" he asked, standing in front of the bakery's back door.

She yanked herself out of her hormone-fueled daze and sprinted for the door.

"Let me open that for you...I'm so sorry," she apologized, fumbling for her keys. "It's just that I was trying to figure out how to lift just one of those bags, and here you are, holding all four of them..."

Damn it, and now she was babbling.

She unlocked and opened the door.

"So, you're from California?" Dane asked as he followed her inside.

"Uh, how did you know that?" she asked, startled. Had Manny told him?

He put the sacks down in her storeroom, which was approximately the size of the walk-in closet in the condo she had shared with Roger, and turned around to grin at her.

She blinked as a rush of heat went through her. No man should be that sexy. It was a crime.

"Your license plates," he said.

"Oh," she said, feeling like an idiot. "Yeah, I'm from the Bay Area. Grew up in the East Bay, but I've been living in the City for the past few years."

"The City—that's San Francisco, right?" he asked as he turned to leave the storeroom.

She nodded and began to follow him back outside.

"So why did you decide to move out here, to the middle of nowhere?" Dane's voice sounded a little muffled as he leaned deep into her car, reaching for the blocks of butter piled on the floor behind her driver's seat.

The urge to tell him the truth was nearly irresistible, but she knew it would be stupid to pour her heart out to a guy she'd just met.

"Just time for a fresh start, I guess." She shrugged and opened her rear passenger door, hauling out the shopping bags holding the containers of cinnamon, active dry yeast, and baking powder.

Okay, maybe that had sounded a little too curt, especially since he had just saved her by dealing with all those heavy bags.

"Besides," she added truthfully, "it would have been another few years before I could even think about opening my own place in the Bay Area. No bank would have loaned me that much money. Things are a lot more reasonable here."

"Manny mentioned you're a friend of his sister," Dane said, his arms piled high with the butter as they headed back inside the bakery.

"Maggie was my boss at Cacao. I really liked working there," Annabeth said with a pang of regret.

The past two weeks had been such a rush of activity, as she settled into the large—enormous, by Bay Area standards—loft apartment over the bakery that had been included in her purchase of the building, that she hadn't had much time to miss Maggie or her old life.

In fact, she had pretty much collapsed with exhaustion every night and fallen asleep right after dinner.

Annabeth had spent most of her time since arriving in Bearpaw Ridge driving around to every restaurant supply warehouse and going-out-of-business sale within a three-hour drive, looking for used equipment and furnishings.

Maggie's older brother Manuel—everyone called him Manny—had been very helpful in getting Annabeth up and running on the business front.

He had helped her get a loan with a good interest rate from the local farmers' bank, though it had terrified her to see her hard-earned savings dwindle down to almost nothing once she handed over the down payment.

Then Manny had helped her score a set of beautiful café tables and chairs at a going-out-of-business sale in Pike's Meadow, just on the other side of the ski resort, and had even gotten the restaurant's owner to deliver them to her.

And he had directed her to the restaurant supply company in Missoula that serviced the ski resort's restaurant, which allowed her to buy her ingredients wholesale.

Their prices were excellent, but her volume of purchases wasn't high enough…yet…for free delivery. She hoped it would be soon.

"So what about you? How long have you been a firefighter?" she asked Dane as she stacked the butter in her big, two-door commercial refrigerator.

She had scored a great deal with the fridge—only two years old and less than half the original cost.

"Since I graduated from high school. It's just a volunteer thing, though," he said. "My real job is managing our family ranch. My dad died in an accident a few years ago, and my mom needs the help. Since the ranch is going to be mine someday, I'm treating this like an apprenticeship. I mean, I've been working with the cattle and doing chores since I was a kid, but Mom's always handled the business end of things—the paperwork, the accounting, and the taxes."

Annabeth groaned in sympathy at the mention of paperwork and taxes.

"That's the part I'm really not looking forward to," she confessed. "It was easier when all I had to do was bake or decorate cakes and Maggie handled all of the paperwork."

"Got that right," he agreed.

They looked at each other, and something hot and urgent flared to life between them. Under the weight of his hazel eyes, Annabeth suddenly felt like she couldn't breathe.

"D-do you want some coffee?" she stammered, not sure if she wanted him to accept the invitation or not.

She was unnerved by how quickly she was becoming infatuated with her fireman hero.

A funny expression crossed his face, as if he were in pain. Migraine, maybe?

"I'm sorry…but I can't," he said, sounding genuinely regretful. "I should be getting home—like you, I have to get up and go to work before the sun rises."

She extended her hand. "Rain check, then. Stop by anytime, and I'll treat you to coffee and the pastry of your choice. And thank you, Dane—you were a real lifesaver tonight."

A jolt moved up her arm as his strong, callused fingers closed around hers.

He felt it, too—she saw his eyes widen at their contact.

"Anything to help a damsel in distress," he said, his tone light.

He didn't let go of her hand.

They stood there, looking at each other, neither of them willing to be the first to move away.

Finally, Dane cleared his throat.

"Good night, Annabeth," he said softly, releasing her hand at last. "Sweet dreams."

Even after the door closed behind him, she could still feel his touch, lingering against her skin.

She suspected that her dreams tonight were going to be *very* sweet.

3
KISSED

The sensible thing for Dane to do would have been to stay away from the bakery until his bear forgot about the whole "fated mate" nonsense.

Unfortunately, he couldn't stop thinking about Annabeth. The way her eyes lit up when she smiled. The irresistible fragrance of healthy woman mingled with vanilla and spice.

And the feeling of sheer *rightness*, of the universe clicking into place when he had touched her.

Damn it. What was he going to do? The longer he went without seeing Annabeth, the more she occupied his every spare thought.

"Dane, are you going to finish filling in that calving spreadsheet sometime this afternoon, or would you like to daydream a little longer?" asked his mother with wry good humor.

Dane, jolted out of his thoughts, jumped a little. He hadn't heard Elle Swanson enter the Grizzly Creek Ranch's office.

Mom was kind and loving but had ruled her family with a firm hand, which was a good thing, considering the idiot antics that a horde of five shifter boys could get up to.

"I'm almost done," Dane assured her.

Feeling guilty, he turned his attention back to the computer's screen. It had been a good spring on the ranch so far, with most of their cows bearing healthy calves.

But Mom wasn't going to let him off that easily.

"So, Evan tells me that you've gone all…what was the term he used?" she asked herself, and Dane braced himself. "Ah, yes, 'googly-eyed' over that pretty little baker in town."

"I haven't," he protested, even as the rising heat in his face betrayed him. Not that he'd ever been able to keep a secret from his mother.

"Really?" she asked skeptically, and he could feel her eyes looking straight into his soul.

"Uh, she's great," he blurted out. "I mean, she's a really good baker. Have you tasted her cinnamon rolls? I just stopped by to see if she needed any help…"

Dane stopped speaking, aware that he wasn't making things any better for himself.

"Oh, Dane, sweetheart." Mom sighed and sat down in the office's other chair. "Not again! You know she's not one of *us*. Not a shifter. And after what happened with poor Tanya…"

As if he needed the reminder!

He had been thinking about Tanya a lot this past week, trying to come to terms with his old pain and feelings of guilt.

"I know," he said tightly.

He knew that Mom meant well. But she didn't understand what was happening with Annabeth.

Then again, neither did he. Even if his bear was dead-certain that Annabeth Jones was their fated mate.

"Just…be careful, honey. I don't want you to get hurt like last time," Mom said softly.

Too late, he thought. The scents of cinnamon and vanilla had already gotten under his skin.

"Hey there, Annabeth," called Dane from the front of the bakery on the following Monday afternoon. "Need a hand?"

Annabeth had heard the front doorbell as she staggered in through the back door, her arms laden with a huge twenty-pound block of butter, and she realized with a jolt that she had left the storefront unlocked when she left after lunch.

That would have been disastrous in San Francisco. But luckily not here, where people didn't even bother to lock their cars most of the time.

"Be there in just a moment!"

Oh, thank God, she thought with complete sincerity. *My hero has arrived!*

Annabeth had just returned from her weekly shopping run to the restaurant supply place and was unloading her car. The butter was the last of the smaller items, and she was bracing herself to drag the first of the fifty-pound flour bags out of her trunk.

She dumped the butter in the refrigerator, then hurried to the front of the bakery, cursing silently as she bumped her hip—yet again—on the big Hobart floor mixer that always seemed to be in the way.

Annabeth came to a halt when she saw Dane standing in the middle of the deserted dining area.

He was even more attractive than she remembered in his worn jeans and a flannel shirt that emphasized the width of his shoulders and chest.

"Hi, Dane!" She smiled at him, very glad to see him, and not just because of those fifty-pound flour sacks waiting in the back of her Prius.

It had been over a week since he had stopped by to help her unload her car. In her few spare moments, she had wondered if she'd done or said something to drive him away.

"Can I get you a coffee and something to eat?" she asked

"That would be great," he said, dropping down into one of her chairs. "I know you're closed today, but I thought I'd stop by and see if you needed any help. But I can only stay for a few minutes," he added, then yawned. "I have get to the hardware store before it closes."

"I'm really glad you came by," she said as she poured him a mug of coffee from one of the tall Airpot thermal carafes lined up on one side of the counter.

Luckily, she'd brewed a pot for herself earlier today, while she was doing her weekly deep cleaning, and it was still piping hot.

"I've missed seeing you around. I'd been wondering if everything was okay with you."

"It's calving season, and everyone at the ranch is a little short of sleep. Including me," Dane said.

He *did* look tired, she thought.

"I sold out of cinnamon rolls at 2:00 p.m. yesterday," she said, apologetically, as she put a plate with a day-old lemon bar in front of him. "But I'm not complaining—I have to tell you, before opening day, I was terrified that I'd flop big-time and lose all my savings. Now I'm worried I won't be able to keep up with the demand. I had to buy twice as much flour and sugar and butter this week."

He chuckled, a low rumble of sound that went straight to the pit of her belly and kindled warmth there.

"Too much demand is a nice problem to have when you're starting a business," he said, the corners of his eyes crinkling in one of those sexy smiles as he took a big bite of the lemon bar. "We had just the opposite problem a few years ago—our small, family-run ranch couldn't compete with the big beef cattle operations in the Midwest. But now there's a real demand for organic, free-range, grass-fed beef, so we're doing all right again. My brother Thor, who lives in Denver, just got us a contract with the Salt & Bourbon Steak House location there."

"Wow," Annabeth said, genuinely impressed. "I had dinner at Salt & Bourbon in San Francisco for my birthday last year. I nearly fainted when I saw the prices on the menu."

Roger had insisted on taking her there. Luckily, he'd also paid the bill afterwards, since dinner had cost nearly a week's wages for her.

"Yeah, it's definitely a high roller kind of place," Dane agreed. "And this lemon bar is *wonderful*."

Annabeth smiled when she saw that only a few crumbs of the shortbread crust remained on the plate.

She rubbed her hip, which was still smarting. She'd just put a bruise on top of her existing bruises, she was sure of it.

"Hey, are you okay?" Dane sounded concerned.

"Fine," she assured him. "It's just my Hobart. I love it—for one thing, it has a programmable timer, so you can just set it, start it, and go do something else for a while. But whoever set it up put it right in the path between the oven and the front counter. So I bump into it a lot."

Dane thumped his coffee mug down on the table and stood. "That's your big mixer, right? Just tell me where you want me to move it," he said, sounding eager.

He headed behind the counter, pushing open the low, swinging gate that separated the dining area from the working part of the bakery

"Wait—I don't think you'll be able to move it by yourself," Annabeth said, hurrying behind him. "It's so big and heavy—oh."

She halted, awed by the ease with which Dane had lifted the bulky floor mixer. It weighed at least four hundred pounds, but he was holding it without any sign of strain.

"Um, if you could move it two feet to your left..." Annabeth managed.

His muscles were bulging under his shirt, and she wanted to stop and appreciate the sight.

"Here?" Dane asked, after moving several steps.

"Perfect!" Annabeth said and watched Dane lower the huge appliance gently to the floor. "Thank you so much. And how did you *do* that without hurting yourself?"

She could have sworn that he looked panicked for an instant. Then he grinned at her and touched the brim of his cowboy hat.

"Why, ranch work will do that for a man, Ms. Annabeth," he said in an exaggerated drawl. "Nothing like wrestling a bunch of half-grown calves to build up your strength."

"Right," she said, not sure if he was joking.

"...and the presence of a pretty lady to make a man not want to look like a wimp," he added with a wink. "I'd have moved a mixer twice that size just for one of those lemon bars and a smile from you."

Annabeth froze. Was the sexiest man she'd ever met actually *flirting* with her? Fat Bethie?

And if he was, was he doing it just to be polite, or did he really find her attractive?

"If—if you liked the lemon bars, I have a couple left over. I—I could pack them up for you," she stammered.

"I'd like that." The sexy smile was back, and it hit her in the gut with a hot punch. "Annabeth, I told you that you'd have people lining up for those cinnamon rolls, but your lemon bars are running a close second, in my opinion. And I'm glad that your bakery seems to be successful so far."

"I'm thrilled," Annabeth said. "I really thought it would take a lot longer to build a customer base, especially in a small town like this."

"See now, that's where the size of Bearpaw Ridge works to your advantage." His smile widened. "Well, and those free samples you handed out the other morning might have had something to do with Mark, Evan, and me telling everyone we knew that they *had* to try your cinnamon rolls."

"I thought I spotted a few firemen in the line," she said, warmed by his words. "I can't thank you enough, Dane. What you've done for me—"

"Was just a little bit of word-of-mouth advertising to get you started," he interrupted gently. "Your hard work and your talent have done the rest, Annabeth. Everyone's talking about your bakery, and I'm sure you've noticed you're getting a lot of repeat customers."

She nodded. She spent most of the past week dashing back and forth between the front and back of the bakery, programming the mixer or rolling out the next batch of buns, then running to the counter to serve customers.

"I honestly didn't think it was going to be this busy, not this quickly," she said. "I need to find a counter person who can handle the cash register and also serve as a barista. Eventually, I'd like to hire an assistant baker, too, and stock the cooler case with pre-made sandwiches, but that can wait. Right now, I'm going to concentrate on coffee and pastries. And wedding cakes." She glanced at him hopefully. "You wouldn't happen to know someone who's looking for a job?"

"As a matter of fact, I do," Dane said. "My cousin Kayla just graduated from college, and she's back home in Bearpaw Ridge for the summer. She'll be here until grad school starts in the autumn."

"Oh, good," Annabeth said gratefully. "Please tell her to come by, and I'll interview her."

"I'll do that. And I'll ask my mom if she knows anyone who might be able to help you with the baking. She knows almost everyone in this county. In the meanwhile, can I help you unload anything from your car?"

"I thought you'd never ask!" She fluttered her eyelashes at him coquettishly and was rewarded with another laugh.

Just as he had before, Dane effortlessly carried the sacks of flour and sugar from her car to her storeroom in a single trip.

"Dane, you are my hero, and you have just won a lifetime supply of free coffee and pastries," she told him when he had finished.

She clasped her hands over her breast like the heroine of a silent movie.

He laughed. "Better not let word of that offer get around, or you'll have men lined up outside the bakery to do your chores." He paused, and his voice went low and sexy. "Promise me that I'm your one and only, and I'll make sure that you never have to worry about any heavy items."

"You are my one and only, Dane Swanson," she said.

Her tone was teasing, but his words had stirred a primal need deep inside her, and that unsettled her.

He's just joking, she told herself. *Don't take it seriously. You don't want to scare him off, do you?*

"Good," he said, and suddenly his tone sounded anything but joking. "Here's my number."

He handed her a business card, and she glanced down long enough to see a stylized bear paw logo and *Grizzly Creek Ranch* emblazoned on it.

"Call me the next time you go shopping at the restaurant supply place. If I'm not available, I'll send my youngest brother Ash over. He works from home, and you can pay him in cinnamon rolls."

"Just how many brothers do you have, anyway?" she asked, curious to learn more about her knight in a cowboy hat.

"Too many, if you ask my mom," he replied, grinning. "She says she kept trying for a girl past the point of good sense. There are five of us—me, Mark, Evan, Thor, and Ashton." He looked up at the bakery clock with a regretful sigh. "And I really need to get going. Hardware store closes in twenty minutes."

"I'll go wrap up those lemon bars for you," she said and went back behind the counter.

When she returned, she held out one of her to-go boxes to him. "I put in some brownies as well," she said.

On impulse—and because she badly wanted to touch him again, she grabbed his hand when he reached for the box. "Dane, I can't thank you enough. You don't know what it means to me to have a friend in a new place."

Afterwards, Dane told himself that he'd been doing fine until she touched him.

He'd known that dropping by the bakery wasn't a good idea, but he hadn't been able to stop himself. Staying away from her had only gotten more difficult as the week wore on. His bear had gotten increasingly restless and irritable with each passing day.

Dane had tried to remind himself that it isn't smart to get involved with an ordinary human. He remembered every minute of that catastrophic last day with Tanya.

But in the end, he couldn't resist the excuse to drive into town for an errand. And once he was there, he told himself that it couldn't hurt to drop by the bakery for five minutes just to say hi.

And to help Annabeth unload her car. His bear liked that, liked doing things for the woman it considered its fated mate.

The temptation of having her standing so close to him, surrounding him with her scent, and smiling up at him as her fingers wrapped around his, proved to be too much.

With a low growl, he pulled her to him and bent his head. He buried his face against the soft, warm skin on the side of her neck, and inhaled deeply.

"You smell so sweet," he whispered and felt her pulse jump against his lips.

Dane took her into his arms, pressing her soft curves against his chest. She fit perfectly against him. She didn't try to pull away. If anything, she leaned into him.

He wanted her with every bone and sinew in his body and with every inch of his soul.

Urgent kisses sent fire though Annabeth's veins as Dane worked his way up her throat to her mouth. His lips were firm, surrounded by the faint prickle of stubble that caressed her tender skin.

Then his mouth reached her lips in a devouring kiss, and the fire in her veins coalesced into a single point of heat between her thighs.

Annabeth returned his kiss with frantic desire as he took possession of her lips with a thoroughness that left her knees weak and her entire body pleading for more.

She lost track of time, forgot where she was. Forgot that they were standing in front of the bakery's windows, where the entire street could see them kissing.

There was only Dane's warm mouth moving hungrily against hers and the hot, urgent desire pulsing through her body.

She felt his hands pulling up the hem of her T-shirt, then the incredible feeling of his callused palms against the bare skin of her lower back.

Annabeth wanted more, wanted him to touch her everywhere.

Then the doorbell chimed, and Evan Swanson said, "This doesn't look like the hardware store, bro."

Annabeth stiffened in shock, and Dane pushed away from her entirely, looking stricken. "I'm sorry," he said. "I didn't mean to—"

And then he was out the door of the bakery, pushing past his brother to escape.

Annabeth stared after him, feeling shaken and dazed, every inch of her awakened and screaming with desire.

"Sorry," Evan said, even managing to sound sincere. "Dane's always so damned serious, I couldn't help poking him a little when I passed by and saw you two. I didn't mean to send him fleeing into the sunset."

Like his brother, Evan was a tall, strapping, dark-haired specimen of cowboy-hatted manhood. At the moment, he looked embarrassed.

"No, th-that's okay," Annabeth managed, trying to convince herself that it was a good thing they were interrupted, before things got out of control.

But damn, Dane was a good kisser. Better than Roger. Better anyone she'd ever dated before.

If Evan hadn't jolted her back to reality, she probably would have torn Dane's clothes off and had her wicked way with him right here in the middle of the bakery.

Evan sighed. "He's really got it bad for you, you know. I haven't seen him like this in years."

Then he frowned and looked away, as if remembering something unpleasant.

"Really?" Annabeth said, disbelieving.

Dane had it bad for *her?* Tall, gorgeous, unbelievably sexy Dane?

Then she remembered that she was still holding the box of lemon bars and brownies. "Would you give this to your brother, please? He, ah, forgot them."

"Not surprising. I think he got distracted by something even sweeter than whatever you've got in here." Evan inhaled deeply as he took the box from her. "Mmmm, lemon and chocolate? What do I have to do to get a care package?"

Annabeth felt the blush start at her chest and move up over her face in a wave of heat. Even her scalp was burning.

Evan stared down at her, an unreadable expression on his tanned, clean-shaven face. "Promise me that you won't hurt him, Annabeth. Please."

"Why would I want to hurt him? Dane is…well, he's *wonderful.*"

That only made Evan sigh and shake his head. "Our family has some…stuff…going on," he said, vaguely but ominously. "Not everyone can handle it. The last woman Dane was serious about…it didn't end well."

Annabeth blinked, not sure what to make of this odd revelation. "Okay," she said cautiously. "I'll keep that in mind."

4

CONVINCED

For the next few days, Dane tried to lose himself in work. God knew, there was never any shortage of things that needed to be done on a ranch—brush cut, fences repaired, calving, painting, you name it.

And then there were the emergency calls that came in for the fire department—a car accident, a near-drowning, and a kitchen fire.

The car accident was awful—a rollover at high speed on a twisting county road about twenty miles out of town.

Dane, Mark, and Evan managed to extract the victim from the wreckage and call for a Medevac helicopter, but they received the news a few hours later that the critically injured young man hadn't made it.

But even keeping himself busy wasn't enough to keep Dane's thoughts from replaying those few blissful moments in the bakery, when sweet, curvy Annabeth had been in his arms, kissing him just as enthusiastically as he had been kissing her.

It had taken every ounce of his self-control not to push her against the nearest wall and fuck her brains out. He wanted to hear her moan his name, wanted to see her face when he made her come again and again…

He tried to convince himself that he should stay away from her. That she'd break his heart when she finally learned the truth about his shifter side.

But deep in his heart, Dane knew that Annabeth was nothing like Tanya.

Besides, it was already too late. Annabeth was going to break his heart no matter whether he stayed away from her or not.

He wondered if she had a boyfriend, someone she'd left behind. Someone she missed.

And found that the thought of Annabeth in another man's arms…or bed…made his bear seethe with angry jealousy. That surprised him. Dane had never been the jealous type.

When Evan knocked on the door of Dane's house after dinner on Saturday evening, Dane had settled down on his couch and was watching the Utah Jazz versus Denver Nuggets game.

He'd been expecting either Mark or Evan to join him at some point, since they usually hung out together to watch games.

Each of the Swanson brothers had his own house on the ranch, with their widowed mother still living in the big, century-old main house.

The ranch office was located in the main house, as well as the big formal dining room, where the family gathered for Sunday dinners and holidays.

Dane's home was the second-oldest building on the property and had originally been built as a retirement home by the first Swanson to settle in the area, when Dane's great-grandfather had turned the day-to-day operations of the ranch and the main house over to his son.

"So about Annabeth," Evan began, once he'd taken a seat and opened the cold beer that Dane had offered him. "I know what Mom's been saying, but I think you should go for it."

"What?" Dane asked, yanking his attention away from the basketball game.

After catching him kissing Annabeth, Evan had given him plenty of shit over the past couple of days. He sounded completely serious now, though.

"I mean, how many single women are there in Bearpaw Ridge, anyway? Not nearly enough, I'm sayin'. And Annabeth's awesome. I really like her, and I wouldn't mind having her as my sister-in-law. Especially if she brings dessert to Sunday dinners."

Dane stared at Evan, surprised. He had expected his younger brother to repeat the advice that Mom had given him about dating non-shifters.

"In fact," continued Evan, "if you're not going to date her, maybe *I* will. She looks really cuddly, and she smells ni—"

"Shut up," growled Dane. He was up and on his feet in an instant, leaning over his brother's chair. He felt a snarl twisting his lips. "And stay away from Annabeth. She's *mine*."

He stopped speaking, shocked at the violence of his instinctual response to Evan's suggestion.

Evan smirked. "Good. I just wanted to hear you admit it." He slapped Dane's shoulder. "Don't let her get away, big brother."

"Annabeth, please come home. Haven't you punished me enough?" Roger was actually *sobbing* into the phone, and Annabeth felt awful.

She just wanted him to hang up and leave her alone. He'd been stalking her on Facebook, sending dozens of PMs and text messages, and calling her every day since she'd left the Bay Area.

And of course, his phone calls always came at the worst possible moment while she was working. It had gotten to the point where she put her cellphone on Vibrate during work hours, which meant that he filled up her voice mailbox with pleading messages for her to call him back.

Tonight, in a moment of weakness, she had answered her phone when he called after dinner. She was already sorry she'd done it.

"This isn't about punishing you, Roger," Annabeth said, as patiently as she could. "I told you, I'm just getting my new business off the ground. I can't go anywhere for a while."

And I don't want to go back to the Bay Area and deal with you, she thought but didn't say.

Roger was in pain. That much was clear. And she didn't want to hurt him more than he was already hurting.

But how she wished he would just give up and stop calling her! Other people had boyfriends who ghosted them, just stopped calling and coming by. Why couldn't Roger have been one of those guys?

"I want to come out and visit you," he said. "Where did you move to, anyway?"

"Uh…" The thought of Roger coming to Bearpaw Ridge instantly made her feel anxious and panicky. *Don't tell him!*

"It's not a good time," she said quickly. "I'm working fourteen-hour days right now, and I need to focus."

"I can't believe how selfish you're being," he told her, his voice trembling. "I love you, and you just *left*. How could you do that?

I was willing to marry you, and you didn't even give me a chance to say goodbye."

What? He's trying to make this my fault?

Annabeth's irritation boiled over.

"I left you because you broke into Cacao and ruined my work because you were trying to get me fired!" Annabeth snapped. "That's not normal behavior! I've made a new start here, and I don't want to see you."

There was a long silence. Inwardly, Annabeth cringed and waited for the explosion.

And had to remind herself that Roger couldn't do anything to her now. She was 900 miles from the Bay Area, and she'd taken everything she valued with her when she packed up.

"Annabeth, *please*," Roger said, and he sounded like he was about to start crying again. "I'll—I'll sign up for anger management classes. We'll go to couple's counseling. Anything. I'll do *anything* if you just come home."

He paused. Annabeth let the silence stretch between them. She had nothing to say that she hadn't already said.

"And…I never hit, you did I?" he continued, at last, a defensive edge creeping into his tone. "Why are you making such a big deal out of one little incident? Especially when it was *your* fault you made me so mad!"

She choked on the unfairness of that statement.

"You're the best thing that ever happened to me, Annabeth, and I'm sorry I fucked it up. Just come back. Please." She heard him take a shaky breath. "We still have a deposit at the San Mateo Tea Gardens for the wedding. I—I haven't canceled it yet, because I'm hoping...I'm really hoping..."

More sobs.

And instead of guilt, all Annabeth felt was revulsion and resentment that he couldn't just let it go. Accept that they had broken up, that she was gone for good, and find someone else to date.

Until she had come to Bearpaw Ridge, she had never lived on her own.

Before now, she hadn't realized how tense she had been all the time that she'd shared Roger's condo. Living with him had felt like she was constantly walking on eggshells, trying to avoid making mistakes or doing anything that might make him angry at her.

These past few weeks, as hectic as they had been, she had felt like she could finally breathe. And truly *relax*, knowing that the bakery and the apartment were hers and hers alone.

No one yelled at her for leaving her paperwork piled on the coffee table. And she didn't spend all her time worrying about how to avoid offending Roger. Or wondering what punishment he would come up with next.

Maggie had been right about Bearpaw Ridge. People were very friendly here. Everyone said "Hi" when they passed you in the street, and if you were driving, they'd wave at you as they went by.

And best of all, Annabeth's constant gnawing sense of anxiety had dissipated in the clean mountain air.

"Roger, I'm sorry," Annabeth said, as gently as she could. "But it's over. I'm not coming back. You need to move on."

His sobs stopped abruptly, and the silence on the line turned cold.

"You ungrateful little bitch," he said, his tone abruptly filled with loathing. "You think you're going to find someone else? I only fucked you because I felt sorry for you. I tried to help you improve yourself, but you're nothing but a stupid fat bitch and—"

Shocked by his sudden venom, Annabeth disconnected the call.

She stared down at her phone. Her hand was shaking, and she felt like she'd just been punched in the stomach.

The depths of the bubbling pit of resentment and hate lurking just below his handsome surface shocked her to her core.

She had actually felt *sorry* for him!

"How did my man-picker get to be so broken?" she said out loud to her empty apartment.

And if she had been so wrong about Roger, then maybe she needed to take things slow…*really* slow…with Dane.

Dane didn't *seem* like the kind of person who would take away the set of Christmas ornaments inherited from her grandmother and donate them to Goodwill to punish her for breaking one of his rules…but then again, she hadn't expected Roger to do that, either.

5

SCREWED

The day that Annabeth afterwards referred to as her Awful, Terrible, No Good Day began innocuously enough.

She woke up when her alarm went off. After braiding her hair and getting dressed in her chef's whites, she gulped down her breakfast. Then she went downstairs to the bakery to mix her first batch of sweet yeast dough for cinnamon rolls.

While the dough was rising, she prepped lemon bars and pecan-bourbon brownies and stuck them in the oven to bake.

Then it was time to grind and brew the coffee for her customers before the morning rush began.

While the coffee was brewing, she rolled out batches of the sweet yeast dough in long rectangles, slathered them with butter and a thick layer of cinnamon sugar, then rolled each rectangle up into a log before cutting thick slices. The slices were placed side-by-side in a big baking pan.

The cinnamon rolls prepped and starting their second rise, she pulled the brownies and lemon bars out of the oven and put the pans on racks to cool. Then she put the first batch of rolls in the oven, set the timer, and started a batch of cream cheese frosting for the rolls in one of her countertop stand mixers.

In a moment of inspiration, she started a chocolate ganache frosting in her other countertop mixer, for the buttermilk brownie cupcakes that were the next thing on her list.

While those were going, she started the cupcake batter in the Hobart, feeling like she was being super-efficient today.

Five minutes before the bakery was due to open, the lights flickered and went out.

And all of the appliances went silent.

Annabeth ran to the front of the bakery and peered out into the pale gray light of dawn, wondering if the whole town was affected by the power outage. But the streetlights were on, as was the neon sign of the pizza place across the street.

The blackout was limited just to her bakery, it seemed.

Annabeth stood momentarily frozen with horror as she contemplated the disaster. Then she took a deep breath, wiped her hands on a clean towel, and began making an assessment.

The mixers were all dead in the water. But the oven was gas, thank God, so it was still functioning. Only the ignition system and controls were electric, so if she left the cinnamon rolls in the oven, they should finish baking, though she needed to set a timer on her smartphone. And she wouldn't be able to turn off the oven until the power came back on.

She wouldn't be able to make espresso drinks without electricity, but she had two out of her three Airpots filled, and the remaining pot was supposed to be Decaf.

Okay, that's manageable.

The cash register was electronic, but she might be able to get by with a calculator and a pad of paper to record her sales.

Oh, God, I hope that whatever's wrong with the power can be fixed quickly. And cheaply.

Annabeth walked to the front of the bakery and saw that her usual crowd of early birds were already lined up outside her door, including three of the town's volunteer firefighters.

None of the Swanson brothers were around this morning, she saw with disappointment.

She always hoped that Dane would come by for a pastry and coffee. Even just a quick hello and a smile during morning rush would lift her spirits for the rest of the day.

What should she do? On the one hand, she didn't have any lights or power. On the other hand, she did have freshly baked goods and freshly brewed coffee to sell…

"Good morning, everyone," she said as cheerily as she could manage as she unlocked the front door. "I'm having some problems with my equipment, so it's going to be cash only this morning, sorry. But please come in."

All things considered, the first two hours went fairly smoothly.

She received a fair amount of sympathy and understanding nods when she explained why the lights were off and she couldn't accept credit or debit cards today. And her cinnamon rolls sold out quickly, as usual.

Then things began to go downhill. It began with her cellphone ringing. She glanced at it. *Roger*. She hit the Ignore button and went back to her customers.

Then her bakery's landline rang.

"Good morning, Cinnamon + Sugar," said Annabeth. "How may I help you?"

"Hey, Bethie," said Roger, breezily, as Annabeth froze in shock. *How did he get this number?* "I need to talk to you about the deposit we have for the Tea Gardens. I want to—"

"I can't talk. This is a bad time, Roger," Annabeth said, trying to keep her irritation out of her voice. "I'm in the middle of my morning rush."

"Look, what would you think about moving the reception to a restaurant, instead?" Roger continued, ignoring her. "I talked to the manager at Salt & Bourbon, and—"

"What reception? Roger, what the hell are you talking about? I'm not marrying you. Good bye," she snapped, and hung up.

Only to meet Evan Swanson's amused look. He had come in while she was on the phone.

Dane's younger brother was wearing fireman's pants and a sweat-stained T-shirt...and a grin that promised trouble.

"I'm sure Dane will be happy to hear that you're not marrying this Roger person, whoever he is," Evan said.

Annabeth felt her face go hot in embarrassment.

"Uh," she began, and then had absolutely no idea what to say next.

What had Dane told Evan about her?

"Sorry," Evan said quickly. "I just couldn't resist the chance to tease you a little. I wasn't trying to be mean. Honest!"

He was still smiling, an irresistible mixture of charm and good humor.

With an effort, Annabeth suppressed her turmoil from Roger's call, put her hands on her hips, and frowned at Evan with mock sternness.

"I'm glad to hear you say that," she teased back. "Since I only have one cinnamon roll left, and I know that *Mark* would never be mean to me." She smiled at the other Swanson brother, who was standing patiently in line behind Evan. "Would you, Mark?"

He shook his head solemnly. "No, ma'am. Especially not if it would cost me one of your cinnamon rolls." He cuffed Evan lightly on the back of his head. "In fact, I think my little brother needs a little punishment. Why don't you sell *me* that roll and just give him a coffee? Black, no cream or sugar."

Her cellphone vibrated. She ignored it.

"Mark! Not helping!" protested Evan, laughing. "C'mon, Annabeth. I know you're a nice person. You wouldn't punish a man who was kicked out of bed at four a.m. on a 911 call, now would you?"

Her landline rang again.

"Of course not," she said, hastily shoving the cinnamon roll in question into a waxed-paper bag and handing it to Evan. "Sorry, Mark. And excuse me, please."

"Good morning, Cinn—" she began.

"Bethie, I really need to—" Roger said, an edge to his voice.

"Roger, what part of *I'm busy* didn't you understand?" Annabeth snapped and slammed the phone back into its cradle.

"Boyfriend?" Evan inquired, all good humor gone.

Mark, standing next to him, was suddenly looking serious as well. As if her answer mattered to him.

"Ex," Annabeth said in exasperation. "But in denial about it." She sighed and forced herself to smile. "Sorry, Mark, we are now out of cinnamon rolls, and I won't be able to make any more until the power's back on."

A groan rippled down the line of remaining people at the news.

"...but I do have lemon bars and brownies, baked fresh this morning. And plenty of coffee."

Her cellphone buzzed again just as a couple of people left the line, looking disappointed. She glared at it, irritated by Roger's harassment.

As the departing customers opened the door to exit the bakery, Annabeth saw a small dog trot in.

"Excuse me," she said to Mark and dashed around the corner to shoo out the pup.

He went, but she saw him sitting right next to the door and wondered if his owner was one of the customers sitting at the tables.

Her landline rang. With a feeling of dread, Annabeth answered it, wishing the ancient rotary-dial phone had Caller ID.

"Good morn—" she began.

"Bethie, don't you *dare* hang—" snarled Roger.

Annabeth hung up.

All right, I don't care if I can afford it or not, I'm going shopping for a Caller ID-enabled landline phone as soon as the bakery closes today.

She finally got Evan and Mark their coffees to go, apologizing profusely for the interruptions.

With a wistful glance at his brother's paper bag, Mark settled for a couple of lemon bars, and Evan paid for both of them.

As they left, the little dog dashed back inside. Annabeth shooed him back out and turned her attention to her next customer.

It was a woman Annabeth didn't recognize, probably a tourist.

She had bright henna-red hair in a stylish bob and was wearing a lot of makeup and an expensive yoga outfit. The nail polish of her manicure matched her lipstick perfectly.

"Good morning," Annabeth said. "How may I help you?"

She ignored the phone as it began to ring again.

The woman looked around with pursed lips at the meager selection in the display case. "No organic, gluten-free pastries?"

"I'm sorry, but we don't carry any gluten-free items at this time," Annabeth said. "But I use local eggs and hormone-free butter," she added.

"I see," the woman said. Her expression implied she found Annabeth's answer inadequate.

Annabeth looked down and saw the woman was holding the leash of a mid-sized border collie.

"I'm sorry, but no pets are allowed inside the bakery. It's the law," she added, apologetically.

"Argus is not a *pet*," the woman informed her frostily. "He's an emotional support animal. I have a *certificate*, from the emotional support animal registry website!"

Annabeth sighed, too tired to argue. And unsure whether ADA covered access for emotional support animals who came with certificates.

"Well, how about your coffee?" demanded the woman. "Is it at fair-trade? Shade-grown?"

The man standing next to her, Bill Hawkins, who managed the hardware store, rolled his eyes at the question.

"I have no idea, ma'am," Annabeth said honestly.

The bakery phone rang again. This time, Annabeth ignored it. It could go to voicemail.

The woman sniffed in disdain.

"Well then, I guess there's *nothing* here I can eat or drink," she declared in ringing tones.

As she turned on her heel and prepared to march out of the bakery, Annabeth overheard Bill mutter, "Good, there'll be more for us, then."

The woman opened the door, giving the small dog waiting just outside the opportunity to dart back inside.

Argus growled at the smaller dog, which growled back. And then the small dog snapped at Argus. Argus lunged forward, teeth bared, and a cacophony of barks and growls filled the bakery.

The phone began ringing again. Five rings, pause for voicemail. Five rings, pause for voicemail. Rinse, lather, repeat.

Roger *really* wanted to talk to her. Annabeth felt like screaming.

"Stop it!" shrieked the woman. "Make him *stop!* He's hurting Argus!"

Bill moved to help her, catching the smaller dog by its collar. The woman bent, scooped up the cowering Argus, and ran out of the bakery.

"What the hell is an emotional support dog?" Bill Hawkins asked a couple of minutes later as Annabeth wrapped up a lemon bar to go and poured him his usual coffee.

The Airpot sputtered, indicating it was nearly empty. And with the power out, she wouldn't be able to brew any more.

"I have no idea," Annabeth said, feeling frazzled. "But I'm glad she left."

As Bill left, she looked around for the little dog, ready to shoo him out of the bakery yet again.

But he had vanished. *Maybe Argus the Emotional Support dog scared him off, and he's gone for good...*

The bakery phone was still ringing. Roger apparently had nothing better to do today than harass her.

Annabeth heaved a sigh and tried to ignore the persistent sound as her doorbell chimed.

She looked up to see a middle-aged woman with long silver-gray hair braided and wrapped around her head in a coronet, tailed closely by Dane and a tall, athletic-looking dark-haired young woman who bore a distinct resemblance to Dane.

The older woman was carrying a clipboard.

The woman stopped inside the bakery and took a long look around. Then she ignored the line of waiting customers and walked up to the non-functioning register.

"Good morning," she said. "Are you Annabeth Jones, the owner of this bakery?"

Annabeth felt a pang of apprehension at the woman's crisp tone—and official-looking clipboard. She nodded and extended her hand. "Yes, I am."

The woman shook it, and the axe of doom fell. "I'm Diane Felsbach, with the county Department of Health. I'm here to perform the annual inspection of your facility."

6

INSPECTED

Annabeth felt panic racing through her as she remembered the buttercream languishing in the mixer bowls and the fact that both the refrigerator and the freezer had been without power for three hours now.

"I've been trying to call you. I wanted to bring my cousin Kayla by, but then I saw that Diane was in town," Dane said.

His sympathetic expression only made Annabeth feel worse.

"Hi Annabeth!" Kayla said brightly. "Have we come at a bad time?"

The first part of the inspection wasn't actually as bad as Annabeth had been dreading.

She had been a certified Food Safety Manager in San Francisco County for years and was able to answer all of Diane's questions about hygiene and temperature controls and to point to her current food safety certificate, framed and mounted on the wall behind the register.

The bakery had a handwashing sink right below the certificates, with soap in the dispenser and plenty of paper towels as well as a box of food service gloves, so Annabeth knew that she would easily pass that part of the inspection.

Then came the bad part, when Annabeth had to tell Diane about her power outage this morning.

"And you still opened for business?" Diane asked, her dark brows rising as she walked to the back of the bakery, stopping to inspect the dishwasher/sanitizer unit and the dishwashing sink.

She checked off items on her inspection list.

"Well, the pastries were already baked, and the coffee was ready when the power went out," Annabeth said. "My morning turnover is always high, and so I didn't think any of those things was going to be sitting around for very long."

"Hm." Diane made a note and kept walking.

"You're not planning to bake and serve any of *these* items, are you?" asked Diane, coming to a halt in front of the mixers, her pen poised over her clipboard. "How long have they been at room temperature?"

Annabeth shook her head. "About three hours. I just haven't had the chance to dump them yet."

"Good answer. If you dispose of them before I leave the premises, I won't note it in the inspection checklist." Diane scribbled something, and Annabeth breathed a sigh of relief.

"And have you used any products from the refrigerator or freezer since the power went out?"

Annabeth shook her head, bracing herself for the news that she would have to throw everything out. "I've kept the doors closed, so I'm hoping that they're still cold enough."

Both the fridge and the freezer had external digital displays for the temperature, which of course meant that they had gone dark when the power went out.

"Well, I'll have to open the doors to take temperature readings," Diane said, looking sympathetic. "You may not have to toss anything if they are still within the acceptable temperature range...that's assuming you get the power turned on again, quickly."

"Thank you," Annabeth said, pleasantly surprised.

"Look, I know stuff happens," Diane said, still sympathetic. "And from what I've seen so far, your premises look clean, your HACCP plan looks good, and you appear to be generally following good food safety practices." She paused and said more gently. "But I think you know that you're going to have to close your business until you get the power back on."

Annabeth nodded, her heart sinking at the idea of losing sales when she didn't even know how much the repairs were going to cost her.

"We'll have the power back on before the end of the day," Dane said confidently.

He had followed them behind the counter and had been silently observing the course of the inspection.

Meanwhile, Kayla had seated herself at an empty table in the now-deserted café area and pulled out her phone to keep herself occupied until the inspection was over.

"I'll be in Bearpaw Ridge until tomorrow afternoon," Diane told him. "If you really can get the power back on, and if Annabeth is willing to dispose of anything that got outside the safe temperature zones, starting with the stuff in those mixers, I'd be willing to re-inspect the bakery before I leave."

"Oh, thank you," Annabeth breathed.

Diane smiled. "I know a lot of restaurant owners think we're ogres, but we just want to make sure that food is safe to eat. We're willing to work with you if you're willing to correct any violations."

Then the small dog who had been so pesky earlier in the morning emerged from behind a rolling rack and danced happy circles around Diane's feet, sniffing at her ankles and wagging his tail furiously.

The bakery phone resumed ringing.

Diane came to a halt in front of the big stainless steel refrigerator and frowned down at the dog. "Is this your dog?"

Annabeth shook her head.

"No, I've never seen him before," she said, afraid that Diane wouldn't believe her. "He's been hanging around the bakery all morning, and I keep having to chase him out."

"Hm. You do know that no animals except for service animals are allowed in bars and restaurants?"

Annabeth nodded. "I've been trying to keep him out, but he keeps coming back inside anytime someone opens the front door."

Dane reached down and scooped up the dog. He looked at the metal tag attached to the collar.

"Thought I recognized you, you little monster," he said playfully. "It's Alfie, Mrs. Granderson's dog. He's an escape artist and manages to get out of her yard at least once a week. I'll drop him off at the Granderson place as soon as you're done here."

Diane sighed and shook her head but didn't say anything…or write anything on her checklist, to Annabeth's relief.

"I'm going to verify the refrigerator and freezer temps now, and then I'm going to halt the inspection until tomorrow," Diane told her. "As of right now, your bakery is closed for business, and I don't want you to serve any food or beverages until I've had a chance to do another inspection." She handed Annabeth a business card. "If for some reason you can't get the power back on in the next two hours, I want you to call me and let me know. Right now, if I find that your refrigerator and freezer have gotten warmer than the allowable temperature range—"

"I know," Annabeth said sadly. "I'll dump everything."

"Okay. Let's get this done, and then I'll go pounce on my next unsuspecting victim," Diane said with a wry smile.

When Diane had departed, heading for The Bear's Lair Pizza & Pasta across the street, Dane put a sympathetic hand on Annabeth's shoulder.

"Hey, don't look so worried. It's gonna be okay," he told her. "If we can get the power back on, you won't have to throw anything out."

Even through her clothing, his touch felt electric.

Annabeth turned to Dane, who still had Alfie tucked in the crook of his muscled arm. The dog was looking up at him adoringly.

"But how am I going to get everything fixed in time?" she asked in despair. "I mean, I'm grateful for your help with Alfie." The dog wriggled eagerly at the sound of his name. "But in my experience, it usually takes at least a day to even get someone to come out to look at the problem. That's time I don't have, not if I'm going to save the stuff in my refrigerator and freezer."

He squeezed her shoulder.

"No problem," he said confidently. "It just so happens that Fred Barker, who adores your cinnamon rolls, is a volunteer firefighter. He's also a licensed electrician. I'll give him a call right now and let him know that your bakery is out of commission and it's an emergency."

"You really *are* my hero!" Annabeth said, grateful but secretly dreading how much the repairs might cost.

The look that Dane gave her in response fairly sizzled the air between them. Annabeth took a half-step toward him.

Then the bakery's phone started ringing again. Annabeth stared at it in despair. Wouldn't Roger ever stop calling her?

Dane looked at her. "Do you mind?" he asked quietly.

She shook her head.

"Cinnamon + Sugar Bakery," he said cheerfully into the phone. A pause. "She's not available right now. Can I help you with something?" Another pause. "Me? I'm her boyfriend, and you're interrupting us, *if* you know what I mean. Who are *you*?"

Dane laughed at Annabeth's open-mouthed expression as he hung up.

"Evan told me that some guy named Roger wouldn't stop calling you this morning. I guess now he won't be calling back anytime soon."

7
SAVED

Dane was a miracle worker. He made the call to his electrician friend, as promised, and whisked the troublesome Alfie away.

Fred Barker arrived at the bakery within a short time, coinciding with Dane's return from Mrs. Granderson's home minus a small dog.

By that time, Annabeth had managed to scrape out the ruined buttercream frosting into the trash and was tackling the cupcake batter, which was in the Hobart's large, unwieldy mixing bowl.

Dane immediately came to her assistance, effortlessly lifting and tipping the bowl's contents into the trash bin while she scraped it out with a large silicone spatula.

Just how strong is he? Annabeth wondered, admiring the play of muscles in his shoulders and arms.

"Annabeth, this is Fred Barker," Dane said, setting the bowl down.

Annabeth had already recognized the pleasant-looking older man as one of her Tuesday morning breakfast regulars. And he usually came to the bakery on Wednesdays and Fridays when it was his turn to sleep overnight at the fire station.

"I'm really glad to see you, Mr. Barker," she said, extending her hand.

He took it and gave it a firm shake. "Call me Fred." He looked around the bakery as if taking note of each piece of equipment. "Dane told me you were having a bit of a problem with your power. Let's see what I can do for you."

"I appreciate that," Annabeth said.

Fred made a beeline for the large electrical panel on the bakery's back wall and commenced to troubleshoot. It didn't take long.

After poking around a bit, then examining the bakery's equipment more closely, he returned to the panel.

Less than two minutes later, the bakery's lights came back on. Better yet, Annabeth heard the refrigerator's motor start up again and settle into a steady, reassuring hum, joined by the sound of her freezer coming back to life.

She checked the digital thermometer display, located just above the fridge doors, and breathed out a sigh of relief.

Still within the specified temperature range for safe food storage! She wouldn't have to toss anything after all.

Fred came up behind her. "Well, I have good news and bad news for you," he said. "Which do you want to hear first?"

"The good news, please," said Annabeth. "Though I think you've already given it to me." She indicated the fridge, then expanded her gesture to include the overhead lights. "You've saved the day, Mr. Barker."

"I thought you were gonna call me Fred?" He looked abashed at her thanks. "Well, the reason that your power went out is that the circuit breakers were tripped. All I had to do was reset them."

"So everything's okay again?"

"For now," he said. "But that's where the bad news comes in. Your wiring is pretty old, and it was never designed for this kind of load."

"But I was told that this place has always been a bakery," she said with a sinking feeling.

He nodded. "Yes, but it's an old facility, and bakeries didn't have as many appliances and electronics back then. I know for sure that Frank never had fancy appliances like these."

"I know," Annabeth said and couldn't help wrinkling her nose at the memory. "I had to replace almost everything before I opened—that old gas oven looked like it was going to explode at any minute!"

"Yeah, well, you really need circuits rated for a higher amperage to handle this kind of load. You've got a refrigerator, a freezer, that big mixer—" Fred pointed at the Hobart, "—plus those two mixers—" he indicated her countertop stand mixers, "and I saw you also have an espresso machine, a fancy register, and that cooler case in front with the juices and sodas, not to mention all the lights and the HVAC system." He shook his head. "It's just a matter of time before something trips the circuit breakers again, and it's really not safe to be overloading your wiring like this."

"What should I do?" Annabeth asked apprehensively.

"In the short term, try not to run too many things at the same time. In the long term—you need to upgrade your wiring to handle a higher amperage load. This place is wired with old aluminum wiring, and you need copper."

Annabeth swallowed hard and tried to draw comfort from Dane's solid presence at her back. He hadn't said much, but he was there, and his silent support meant a lot to her.

"And how much do you think that will cost?" she asked Fred, dreading his answer.

She had already spent most of her savings on the down payment and start-up costs. She was going to have to put this emergency repair on her credit card and then try to find a way to pay it off quickly.

Fred looked at her for a long moment, and she wondered if her panic showed. Then he smiled gently. "Annabeth, you know, I've been looking at that cake on display in that case over there."

He jerked a thumb at the sample wedding cake she had decorated with fondant and royal icing over stacked foam rounds of graduated diameters, from eighteen inches for the base layer to six inches for the top layer.

"So I'm guessing you do wedding cakes?"

Annabeth nodded. She hadn't received any orders yet in the short time that her bakery had been open, but they had been a staple of her weekly work at Cacao. And decorating cakes had been one of her favorite tasks when she worked for Maggie. It was fun, and the results made her customers happy.

"And how much does one of those cakes go for?"

"That would depend on the number of guests," she answered, puzzled by the turn the conversation had taken. "Bakeries usually charge by the number of servings."

"Say, 500 guests, give or take twenty or thirty?" He was still smiling, the crow's feet deeply carved into the corners of his gray eyes.

She did a quick calculation in her head and gave him the price range.

His eyes widened at the quote.

"It really depends on the decorating scheme," she explained. "Some brides want a relatively plain cake, because they plan to put fresh flowers on each tier and as the topper. Other brides choose something more labor-intensive, like the design on my model cake. That took about two full days to decorate, including making all the rose petals one by one from gum paste and then painting them with pearlescent food coloring."

Bill nodded slowly. "I can see that." He looked at the model cake for a moment longer. Then he seemed to come to decision. "Annabeth, I'll tell you what. My daughter Lisa is getting married mid-July, and her mother and I promised to pay for the wedding cake. So how about a trade? I'll rewire your bakery, and you make and deliver the cake for my daughter's wedding at the Bearpaw Springs Resort on the second Saturday in July. That sound fair to you?"

Annabeth stared at him in shocked gratitude. She couldn't believe her luck—or how kind he was being. She suspected that he was offering her a very generous deal. Maybe he'd guessed that she couldn't really afford an expensive repair right now.

"Mr. Barker, uh, Fred, you have a deal." She extended her hand. "Give me your daughter's phone number or email, and I'll call her tomorrow or the day after to set up an appointment to discuss flavors and what kind of decorations she'd like. I'll make sure that she—and you and your wife—are happy with your cake. And I'll bake the bride and groom a fresh cake for their first anniversary, so that they don't have to save the top layer and put it in the freezer."

"Deal, then." He shook her hand, firmly. "And thank you."

"No, thank *you!*" she countered, smiling.

And included Dane in that smile. He winked at her.

"Well, that's a weight off my shoulders," Fred admitted. "My wife and I thought we'd have to go to one of the bakeries in Missoula—there's only one other bakery that does wedding cakes in this area, and well, we tried one of their cakes at someone else's wedding, and it tasted like one of those supermarket cake mixes. And it wasn't nearly as pretty as *that* cake." He indicated her model with his chin.

"I can't tell you how grateful I am, Mr. uh, Fred," Annabeth said. "From now on, there's a free cup of coffee and a pastry for you anytime you stop in. Thank you, from the bottom of my heart."

His weathered cheeks flushed a little. "It's no problem, really. There are a lot of people in town who would really miss your cinnamon rolls if you had to close down your bakery, Annabeth."

"And thank you, Dane," she said, turning to the big man standing quietly at her shoulder. "Once again, you've saved the day."

Dane looked embarrassed. "It was just a phone call, Annabeth. Fred here is going to be doing the actual work."

"Still," Annabeth insisted firmly. "I wouldn't have known who to call."

"My boys and I will get started on the rewiring project next week," Fred offered. "We can do it in the evenings, so that you won't have to close shop."

He waved off Annabeth's further attempts to thank him.

"Just save one of those cinnamon rolls for me tomorrow morning," he said cheerfully as he left the bakery.

When Annabeth called Diane a few minutes later and told her that everything was up and running again, the inspector said, "That's great!" She paused. "Look, I know you probably want to reopen first thing tomorrow morning, so why don't I come by when I finish up here…say, in an hour?"

"Thank you, I'd really appreciate that, Diane," said Annabeth, with a fresh spurt of stress, remembering the state of the mixers.

Only an hour to get ready for an inspection!

Diane had been very kind, but still, Annabeth wanted to make sure that her bakery passed inspection with flying colors this time.

"Do you want me to tell Kayla to come back tomorrow for her interview?" asked Dane when Annabeth had finished her call.

"Oh God, Kayla," Annabeth exclaimed, mortified. "I forgot all about her!"

Then an idea struck her.

Tailed by Dane, she hurried to the front of the bakery. Kayla was still sitting at one of the tables in the now-deserted café area, her thumbs flying over the keyboard of her phone.

"Kayla, I'm so sorry to keep you waiting. My mornings aren't usually this, um, interesting."

"Hey, no problem," Kayla said, quickly tucking her phone into the pocket of her bright blue hoodie.

"I have a proposal for you," Annabeth said. "Diane is coming back to finish her inspection now that the power's back on. She'll be here in an hour."

Annabeth had to take a deep, calming breath at the thought of everything she wanted to do before Diane returned.

"If you're willing to help me get this place ready for round two of the inspection, I'll hire you on the spot. Minimum wage plus tips."

She waited for Kayla's answer, hoping that Dane's cousin wouldn't turn her nose up at the "minimum wage" part.

But Kayla only grinned and stood. She was tall and athletic-looking, with a tanned, healthy complexion, hazel eyes, and a freckled nose.

"I'd love to work here, Annabeth. Once that espresso machine is running again, I'll be raking in the tips," she said confidently. "What would you like me to do first?"

Annabeth breathed a sigh of relief. "If you could start by sweeping up all the flour in the back, especially around the Hobart, that would be great. Brooms and mops and cleaning supplies are kept in the storage closet next to my office, all the way in the back."

"I'll help too," Dane offered. "It's my day off, and I was going to ask if you wanted to go out for lunch." He quirked a smile, waving off her attempt at thanks. "The sooner we can get Diane's inspection over and done with, the sooner I can introduce you to the wonder that is a Dancing Cow burger."

Kayla stopped in her tracks. "If he's taking you to Dancing Cow, make him buy you a milkshake too. The Salted Caramel and Speculoos one with the Belgian cookie crumbs is my favorite."

"Actually, I was going to recommend the huckleberry shake, since that's a real local treat," Dane said.

"Huckleberry's good, too," Kayla agreed. "But the Speculoos one is *amazing*."

8
SUPPORTED

"I didn't have any doubts that Diane would give you a passing grade once we got the power back on," Dane said two hours later.

The bakery had been scrubbed from top to bottom, and Diane had come and gone.

To Annabeth's relief, the bakery had easily passed the reinspection, and she was cleared to reopen in the morning.

While Kayla had swept up all of the spilled flour and crumbs, then mopped the linoleum floor, Dane had helped Annabeth clean the mixer bowls and attachments. Then they had wiped down all of the stainless steel countertops.

"Are you ready for lunch?" he asked.

"Am I ever!" she answered.

After the nonstop crises so far today, she felt completely wrung out. And ravenous.

She added, "And please let me treat you both. After all the help you've given me today, it's the least I can do."

Dane looked dismayed, and Annabeth realized that he had meant to ask her out on a date.

I am such an idiot!

But it was too late to withdraw her invitation to Kayla.

Kayla threw Dane a meaningful look, then said, "That's really nice of you, Annabeth, but I can't. I told some of my friends I'd meet up with them after my interview here. You and Dane go ahead, and I'll see you in the morning. What time would you like me here?"

"At 4:45, so that you can get the coffee going for the Airpots," Annabeth said, relieved that Kayla had offered her a graceful way out. "We open at 5:00, and there are always at least a few people waiting in front of the door by then."

"Okay, see you bright and early tomorrow," Kayla said cheerily and left with a wave.

"I'll drive," Dane offered as Annabeth turned off the bakery's lights.

As promised, the burgers were delicious, and the milkshakes even more so.

Best of all was the company.

If Annabeth had been nursing a crush on her gorgeous cowboy before, his actions today, which could have easily been one of the worst days of her life, had made her fall in love with him.

He made her feel good. Like someone genuinely cared about her. Like she wasn't completely on her own in this new place.

"So about this Roger guy…" Dane began when they had ordered their burgers and shakes and were seated outdoors on the Dancing Cow's patio.

Annabeth was still dressed in her chef's pants and a short-sleeved, tunic-like chef's coat. She wished she had thought about going upstairs to her apartment to change clothes before they left for lunch. But Dane didn't seem to mind, so she tried not to worry about her attire.

It was a beautiful late spring afternoon, sunny and warm, with just a few fluffy white clouds over the mountains that surrounded Bearpaw Ridge.

Dancing Cow Burgers was located by the side of the highway on the outskirts of town, which meant that diners on the patio were often treated to the sight of grazing deer or elk in a nearby meadow.

Today, a flock of sandhill cranes, tall and elegant in fawn brown plumage with long necks and scarlet caps on their heads, stalked slowly through the meadow.

Annabeth wrinkled her nose. "Do we have to talk about him?"

Dane leaned forward on his elbows, and Annabeth covertly admired the play of muscles in his thick forearms. "I just want to know—was he always that much of an asshole?"

"Not at first. And he can be really charming when he wants to be, so it took me a while to figure that part out," Annabeth replied unhappily. "Also, everyone I knew—except Maggie—thought he was a great catch, so looking back, I just sort of ignored a lot of the early warning signs, because I didn't want them to be true."

She sighed and met Dane's eyes. "Look, Dane, you have no idea how much I appreciate what you did for me today—and all the help you've given me over the past few weeks. I'm—I'm not used to getting help. But you make me feel like you've got my back, and I can't describe what a great feeling that is."

Dane's face flushed under his tan. He reached across the table to take her hand, and she felt the same exciting jolt of desire that she had felt before.

"Why wouldn't I help you out?" he asked, sounding puzzled. "And it's all been little stuff, anyway."

He wasn't just good-looking, he was thoughtful, kind, and protective.

And she wanted him so badly that it was taking every ounce of her self-control not to get up and go sit on his lap.

Annabeth shook her head. "It wasn't little stuff, not to me. You know, while we were driving here, I was thinking about how amazed I was when you just jumped in to help me as soon as you saw I was in trouble."

Dane scrutinized her, then heaved a sigh. His fingers tightened around her hand. "Annabeth, you're talking like no one's ever taken care of you before."

She shrugged. "My mom encouraged independence. She had to, because she was usually working two jobs after my dad left. I've always taken care of myself."

"And what about Roger? Didn't he take care of you?" Dane demanded.

He had a funny look on his face as he asked it, though, as if something tasted bad.

"Well, he paid for a lot of things," Annabeth admitted. "Because he earned more money than I did."

Dane's oh-so-kissable lips thinned at her answer. "So if he'd been here today instead of me, what would he have done?"

Annabeth considered the answer and sighed. She didn't really want to talk about Roger while she was having a nice lunch out with Dane.

Roger would have expected her to fend for herself no matter what happened, and she would have had to make sure that *his* needs were taken care of, no matter how stressful or exhausting her own day had been.

"He would have paid for the rewiring," she said finally. "But he would have blamed me for not realizing that there was a problem during the prepurchase inspection before I made the down payment on the bakery. And it *was* stupid of me not to know that." Annabeth sighed. "He probably would have insisted that I demand a refund on the inspection fee."

She wrinkled her nose, happy that she wouldn't have to do that. Or have to listen to Roger ranting about how incompetent Annabeth was and how she always let people take advantage of her.

Bearpaw Ridge was a small town, and as a newcomer, the last thing she wanted to do was raise a stink about something that she should have known about, anyway.

"I don't think you're stupid for assuming that since Frank was able to run all his bakery equipment, you'd be able to as well," Dane said, looking angry.

"Well, I did buy those new KitchenAid mixers and a new refrigerator and oven, and the coffee delivery guy offered me a low-cost lease on that espresso machine that I couldn't resist," Annabeth argued. "I should have known it might be too much for the wiring in a building as old as this."

That only made Dane shake his head in vigorous denial.

She sighed. "Maybe Roger was right. I still have a long way to go before I'm any good at…well, anything."

Dane's piercing hazel eyes widened. "What? Because you don't know much about wiring and electricity?" His mouth twisted wryly as he lowered his voice to a stage whisper. "This is the part where I confess that I don't know much about them either, but I think you're pretty much perfect, in all other ways."

He sounded absolutely sincere. Annabeth stared at him. "But—there are so many things—I mean, I never managed to do everything on the list…"

Her voice trailed off at Dane's look of confusion. "List? What list? Annabeth, what are you talking about?"

Regretting that she'd blurted out that humiliating detail, she twiddled a cooling French fry between the fingers of her free hand rather than meet his gaze.

"Yeah, well, Roger would—he used to email me lists of things I needed to do if I wanted to be an acceptable girlfriend."

"What?" Dane exploded. "Jeez, he really is an asshole! No wonder you left him!"

Annabeth's cheeks grew hot as she reduced the French fry to a flattened length of mush between her fingertips.

"So tell me," Dane said, his tone not quite conversational. "What kind of things is a so-called *acceptable girlfriend* supposed to do?"

Annabeth found it all too easy to remember. She ticked the points off on her fingers as she recited:

"Before I left for work in the morning, I was supposed to send him a list of what chores I was going to do that day and then update him on my progress before he got home from work.

"I wasn't supposed to make any noise in the mornings, because I had to get up at 2:30 a.m., but he didn't have to be at work until nine.

"I had to let him know what I planned to cook for dinner, so that he could make sure it was something that he liked.

"I had to hand over my paycheck to pay for my share of the household expenses. I wasn't allowed to spend more than $150.00 a month on stuff for myself, like clothes and makeup, and I had to keep a spreadsheet so he could track my spending."

As she spoke, she noticed Dane's expression growing more and more outraged.

"What kind of chores were you supposed to do, on top of a full day's work at your job?" he asked, his voice low now, with the edge of a growl.

"But Roger's job was really stressful, and he worked long hours..." Annabeth began, yielding to her old need to justify his demands.

With an effort, she stopped speaking. It *hadn't* been fair, and she knew it.

Dane squeezed her hand comfortingly.

Why had she mentioned those lists in the first place? It was stupid and in the past, and despite his self-control, she could tell that Dane was getting upset.

"And what would happen if you forgot something on his list or didn't do it the way he liked?" Dane asked.

Annabeth took a deep breath before answering. "He—he would break something that belonged to me, or he'd donate it to Goodwill. Last year, he took away the birthday present he'd given me…it was just a stupid pendant, but…" She stopped, fighting for control. After all this time, she hadn't expected that memory to hurt as much as it did. "I—I finally couldn't take it anymore, so when Maggie told me about the bakery here…"

"Oh my God." Dane stared at her like she had just grown a second head.

With an odd jolt halfway between terror and desire, she noticed that his hazel eyes had lightened to green-gold. They blazed with strong emotion.

Deliberately, he took her other hand and leaned forward across the table.

"Annabeth," he said, his voice even lower and hoarser than before. "You are amazing, and perfect just the way you are. I promise you I will never, *ever* make a list. And if I ever meet Roger, I'm going to tear his face off."

His fingers tightened around hers, and she felt a rush of heat at his unexpectedly fierce protectiveness, even as his threat chilled her.

It was the absolute certainty in his voice that made it so scarily believable, she decided.

"Dane," Annabeth said, her throat tight with gratitude and affection and wonder and a hundred other emotions trying to rush out of her at the same time.

She raised his hands to her lips and kissed each large, rough knuckle in turn.

As her lips touched his skin, she gazed up at him through her eyelashes and saw his fierce anger turn to a hunger that burned just as hot.

"Roger is miles away in California," she whispered. "And I'll never have to see him *or* his lists again."

Dane gave her a slow smile that took her breath away. "Are you finished with lunch?"

She bent her head and softly kissed the inside of his wrist. His pulse jumped against her lips. "I believe I am."

"Good," he said, his voice still gravelly. "I'd like to take you home now."

9

SEDUCED

Dane didn't let go of her hand while he drove them back to her place.

Annabeth studied his profile, admiring the strong line of his jaw and chin as his thumb inscribed delicious promises against the sensitive skin of her palm with slow, sensual circles.

He had called her *beautiful* and *amazing*. And he had sounded like he meant it.

How had she gotten so lucky?

By the time he parked at the delivery entrance behind the bakery, the place between her legs was throbbing with urgent heat.

Neither of them spoke as they left his truck, but the atmosphere sizzled between them, heated with anticipation.

Annabeth slipped her hand into Dane's again as soon as he had closed the driver's side door. Their fingers intertwined, she led him up the rickety wooden stairs behind the bakery to her apartment.

She paused on the landing in front of her door, digging in her purse for her keys.

She knew she was an outlier for always locking her door in this small town, but she had found it surprisingly difficult to break the habits of a lifetime lived in the urban environs of the San Francisco Bay Area.

"Annabeth," Dane said in a hoarse, desperate voice and grabbed her shoulders. "I really want to—I *need*—"

Annabeth forgot about her keys and tilted her face up to him, her heart pounding in anticipation. She felt his fingers slide into her hair, cradling her face between his large palms.

Dane bent his head, and she parted her lips, longing for the touch of his mouth against hers.

In contrast to his previous kiss, which had been gentle and exploratory, his mouth this time devoured hers hungrily as he pressed Annabeth up against the door of her apartment, in clear view of the parking lot below.

As his lips caressed hers, firm and urgent, his tongue pushed into her mouth, teasing and caressing and taking possession of her.

Annabeth squirmed under the sensual assault and rubbed herself shamelessly against him, standing on tiptoes to wind her arms tightly around his neck, enjoying the feeling of the broad, hard planes of his chest against her breasts.

She kissed him back with an urgency that matched his, torn between savoring his intoxicating kisses and wanting more… the kind of *more* that generally happened on a bed.

"Oh God, you smell so good," Dane groaned, pulling away at last.

She dug her fingers into his shoulders, protesting the loss of contact and trying to pull him close again.

She pressed her hips against him and felt the hard bulge of his desire pushing urgently against the soft curve of her belly.

He was driving her crazy, and she wanted every big, hard, scrumptious inch of him. Badly.

Dane buried his face in her neck, inhaling deeply. "So sweet…I could eat you up."

She felt the light rasp of his stubbled cheek and chin as he kissed and nipped the tender skin there.

"Promises, promises," she panted, letting her head thump back against the unyielding wood of her front door. She offered her throat to him, feeling sharp jolts of pleasure zing through her with every urgent caress.

"You have no idea," he growled.

Annabeth clutched at him with one hand and resumed digging in her purse with the other. Damn it, why couldn't she leave her doors unlocked like every other crazily trusting person in this town?

Her fingers finally encountered cold metal. *Victory!*

"Dane, why don't you come in?" she managed, turning in his arms.

He didn't let go, just allowed her to rotate in his embrace to unlock her door while he pressed himself against her back.

She felt him lift the heavy, curling mass of her hair and kiss the back of her neck. Pleasant shivers raced down her spine to the pit of her belly, and she had a sudden, vivid fantasy of letting Dane fuck her like this, from behind, her cheek pressed against the door, his big hands cupping her breasts…

…just like *that*.

She gasped as his thumbs brushed over her nipples. Even insulated by two layers of fabric, she felt the electric current of desire arrowing right between her legs.

"God, don't stop," she managed, just as the door swung inwards, sending her staggering.

But Dane's freakish strength saved them both as he caught her and pulled her back against him.

"You like that?" he breathed.

He caught the edge of her ear delicately between sharp teeth as his thumbs made another pass over her nipples.

Annabeth whimpered, arching in his arms.

"Good," Dane said. "Because I want to touch you everywhere. Kiss you everywhere. *Lick* you everywhere. Do you want that, too, Annabeth?"

"Yes. Please, Dane," she begged. She wanted everything that this big, wonderful man was willing to give her.

"Good."

His hands left her breasts, and she inhaled, ready to protest.

Then she felt his callused palms slide under her chef's coat, pushing it up, caressing the bare skin of her waist and stomach before rising to push the bottom edge of the bra up and over the swell of her bosom, freeing her.

"God, you're beautiful, Annabeth," Dane said with mingled reverence and desire as he cupped her bared breasts and gently lifted them. "So beautiful."

He began to tease her nipples with his thumbs, each caress sending a rush of fresh heat and exquisite pleasure through her as they hardened into yearning points.

All the while, he continued to kiss her neck and nibble her ears and murmur compliments.

He was driving her crazy with desire. She wanted him so badly that she thought she would die—or at least scream—if she couldn't get him out of his Wranglers soon.

And they hadn't even made it as far as her living room. They were standing in her entry hall, the front door still open behind them.

"Dane," she gasped. "Won't you come in?"

He chuckled, his breath hot against the back of her neck.

"Why, Annabeth, I'd *love* to," he replied, wickedly, and she giggled at the unintended double entendre.

But he released her and let her close the door and lead him into her apartment, though she could still feel the imprint of his touch everywhere he had caressed her.

Annabeth stopped in front of her couch, suddenly aware that her place looked like a tornado had hit it. Her coffee table was piled with paperwork and manila envelopes jostling against her laptop.

Piles of clean, folded laundry took up half of the couch.

And she hadn't bothered to make her bed, since she hadn't been expecting anything but a normal work day today when her alarm went off hours before dawn.

"Dane, I'm sorry about the mess," she began, but saw he was looking around with approval.

"This looks like a great place to live," he commented.

"It is. I really like it," she replied. "I didn't have any furniture to move, so I had to buy stuff, mostly used. The mattress is new, though," she added hastily, then felt her face grow hot.

Dane chuckled. "I see you've got your priorities straight."

She laughed, too.

"I've never lived in a place this big," she confessed. "It's taking me a while to furnish it."

The apartment took up the entire second floor of the two-story brick bakery building. By Bay Area standards, it was enormous, with high ceilings that looked a hundred years old, and two big skylights.

It was designed like a loft, with a great room that served as a combined living room, dining room, and bedroom.

Tucked away along one wall was small, old-fashioned kitchen with ancient appliances including a fridge that looked like it might be older than Annabeth's grandma.

A long, granite-topped breakfast bar with four antique brass-and-leather stools divided the kitchen area from the living room area.

Her queen-sized bed and nightstand were shoved against the wall behind the large square formed by a large sectional sofa with a chaise.

One of the apartment's two doors led to a large walk-in closet. The other door opened onto a generously sized tiled bathroom, which had an antique claw-foot tub with attached shower and an old-fashioned toilet with the water tank perched several feet above.

Annabeth turned to face Dane. "Can I get you some cof—"

His arms came around her again, and then his mouth was covering hers, hot and insistent.

Kissing frantically, they stumbled toward the couch. Annabeth swept out an arm and sent the piles of clean clothing tumbling to the floor an instant before Dane drew her down onto his lap.

His hand slipped back under her blouse, and he caressed the small of her back with slow circles. The heat of his touch felt like a brand against her bare skin

She settled herself on his hard thighs and eyed the erection pushing at the front of his jeans. She wanted to reach out and put her hand over the bulge and stroke it, but felt inexplicably shy.

"You're a sweet lapful, like I knew you'd be." He grinned, but his hazel eyes burned.

Annabeth's heart leapt. "I actually fantasized about doing that while we were having lunch," she confessed, and he laughed.

"Great minds think alike?" he joked, just before she wriggled forward a couple of inches and straddled his lap properly.

His leg muscles were rock-hard against the insides of her thighs, and she liked the way it felt.

She was still wearing her loose chef's trousers. With his jeans, both of them had way too many layers of clothes between them.

Annabeth took his face in her hands and kissed him.

He returned her kiss with enthusiasm, letting their tongues engage in an urgent, thrusting dance of courtship. When she finally moved away from his mouth, they were both panting.

She placed tiny kisses along the strong line of his jaw, reveling in his spicy scent, and he tilted his head back, eyes closed, baring his throat in a silent plea.

Annabeth yielded to her desire to nibble on him and traced the line of his pulse with her lips and tongue. He smelled good, like clean male, and just the faintest hints of smoke and aftershave.

With shaking fingers, she reached to pull his shirt out of his jeans, letting her fingertips brush the warm, smooth skin of his torso. She undid one shirt button and stopped, waiting for permission to continue.

He opened his eyes. "Don't stop now," he said hoarsely.

10
THWARTED

She fumbled open the rest of his shirt buttons with desperate haste, dying to see what sexy things lay beneath the concealing fabric.

Dane's chest and torso were beautiful, big and hard with sculpted muscle, his pectorals lightly dusted with dark hair that narrowed to a thin line down his belly before disappearing into his pants.

He was so very responsive to her touch. She liked how his breath caught when she brushed one of his cinnamon-colored nipples with the edge of her fingernail.

It tightened to a hard point as she played with it, and Dane groaned, his muscles tensing beneath her.

His movements brought the hard ridge of his erection against her crotch. A sharp jolt of pleasure wrung a gasp from her.

Experimentally, she rolled her hips, rubbing herself shamelessly against him.

It felt good, so *very* good, even with both of them still wearing pants...

"Annabeth," Dane groaned, after a few pleasurable moments. "Stop...*please*. Or I'm going to come."

With an effort, she stopped moving her hips. God, he looked so sexy like that, with his hair tousled and his shirt open and his expression desperately hungry.

Hungry for *her*, extra pounds and all. The way he was looking at her made her feel like the most beautiful woman in the world.

"Don't you want to come?" She moved her hands lower, toying with his belt buckle.

Annabeth wanted see all of him now. She wanted to wrap her fingers around his hard cock and see if she could make him lose control.

Wanted to see him lost in the throes of pleasure that *she'd* given him.

"Yes, but first, I want to taste you," he said hoarsely. "Please."

"Yes," said Annabeth. "Oh, yes."

"But first..." He gave her a slow smile that did things to her insides. *Nice* things. "I'd like to see those gorgeous breasts of yours." He paused and added, with a wink, "Pretty please?"

That made her laugh again. She had always felt a little tense while having sex with Roger, worried that she wasn't doing something right or was not reacting in a way that he would like.

But making out with Dane was *fun*, hot and sexy and humorous. And she hadn't worried about anything—his kisses had driven all rational thought out of her mind, until all she wanted to do was *feel*.

Slowly, deliberately, she unbuttoned her chef's coat, watching Dane's expression as she revealed more and more of her breasts, until finally, she slid the halves over her shoulders and let the coat drop to the floor at Dane's feet. Her bra, still shoved out of place, followed, leaving her bare to the waist.

Then Annabeth perched on Dane's lap, watching his pupils dilate as he looked at her.

"Beautiful," he breathed and leaned forward to place two quick kisses on the tips of her breasts.

His mouth lingered as he began to worship her with his lips and tongue, kissing the soft curves, teasing her sensitive nipples to hard, aching points.

It was heaven. It was hell. She squirmed and panted as his hands settled firmly on her hips and he worked her over.

"I want to hear you," he said, just before his teeth closed gently over one hard nipple.

Annabeth whimpered in response, unable to control herself. She thought she might come just from the intense sensation.

"Yeah, like that," Dane whispered. "I love it when you make noise for me."

She clutched at his shoulders and threw her head back, her body on fire for him.

"I want to make you come," Dane told her in a low, intense voice, in between playful, nipping kisses that teased and made her want more. "I want to taste you and hear you scream my name."

She nodded frantically, so turned on now that it hurt with a throbbing ache between her legs.

"Please," she begged. "Please."

"Stand up and take off your pants," Dane ordered.

Annabeth wriggled eagerly off his lap. Her knees felt rubbery, and her heart was pounding as if she'd just run up five flights of stairs.

"Slow down, please," he said, as she unbuttoned the waist of her pants and shoved them down her legs with frantic haste.

"What?" Annabeth asked, startled.

Dane leaned back and folded his hands behind his head. He grinned up at her. "I'm enjoying the show."

And she liked the idea that he enjoyed looking at her. So she made an effort to step slowly out from the pants crumpled around her ankles.

Her breath catching with anticipation, aware of his burning green-gold gaze on her, Annabeth reached down slowly and hooked her thumbs under the top of her panties.

Slowly, teasingly, she slid her underwear down her thighs to her ankles. She stepped out of her panties, leaving a crumpled scrap of aqua cotton and lace on her rug.

"*Very* nice." Dane stretched out a big hand, then tugged her down onto the couch next to him. "Make yourself comfortable, beautiful…maybe scoot a little closer to the edge? Oh, that's good." His voice was low and rough, sending a primal thrill through her.

With a smooth movement, he slid off the couch and knelt before her. "Open your legs for me."

Annabeth did it and felt him kiss the inside of her left knee.

Dane kissed his way up the inside of her thighs, making her squirm with impatience and desperate need.

She jumped as he blew lightly across her aching, sensitized folds.

"You smell even more wonderful than I thought. You're driving me crazy, Annabeth. All I can think about is doing this—"

Annabeth gasped sharply as the tip of his tongue circled her swollen clit in a slow swirling caress.

"Oh, God," she said, fervently, as he set to work.

Dane was very, *very* good with his mouth. In no time, he had her writhing and pleading with him as a coil of pleasure began to tighten between her legs.

On the rare occasions when Roger had tried giving her oral, it had never felt like *this*, wild and urgently ravenous.

She had always tensed up, afraid of taking too long to come, worried about the fact that she knew Roger didn't really like to use his mouth on her and that he'd be upset if he thought she wasn't sufficiently grateful.

But Dane—Dane plunged right in, kissing, licking, sucking every secret part of her. He fucked her enthusiastically with his tongue, teasing her with the thick, slippery length until she was begging.

And the entire time, he looked like he was enjoying doing this to her almost as much as she was enjoying having it done.

He brought her right up to the edge—then stopped. His big hands on her thighs kept her a tantalizing distance from his mouth as she arched against the sofa cushions and tried to grind herself against him.

She made an inarticulate sound of protest, desperate for release.

"Do you want to come now, Annabeth?" His voice was husky and very low. And his eyes were nearly gold now.

He blew a teasing puff of air against her, and she moaned, nodding frantically.

"Will you scream my name when you do?" he asked.

"Y—yes," she managed.

"Good," he purred. "And if you don't manage it this time, then I'll just have to try again."

He bent his head and took her clit between his lips, working it with his lips and tongue.

She fell over the edge into climax, sobbing his name as sweet, almost unbearable waves of pleasure wracked her for long moments.

Dane's caresses became lighter and more lingering, drawing out her pleasure as she began to come down from her orgasm.

Limp with pleasure and floating, she was dimly aware when Dane moved up onto the couch next to her.

"Did you like that?" he asked softly.

Annabeth smiled and curled up against his side. She couldn't remember the last time she'd been so happy.

"Mmm, better than chocolate," she assured him.

She felt so relaxed that it was difficult to talk.

"I'm glad. Because you are amazing and beautiful," Dane said, putting his arm around her. "And we're not done yet. I want to see you come again…and maybe again after that."

That sounded wonderful…once she found the strength to sit up again.

"But what about you?" Her gaze strayed down to the telltale bulge at his groin, and guilt jabbed like a cold finger through the warm golden haze surrounding her. "You didn't get anything out of this."

"That's not true," he said. "I loved tasting you and watching you come, Annabeth. You're sweeter than honey. But you don't have to—"

"I *want* to," she said, breathlessly, surprised to find it was true.

She put her hand over the long ridge of his undiminished erection and stroked him, tracing his hard length through the thick denim. It was immensely gratifying to hear his breath hitch in response.

"My turn. Or should I say, *your* turn?"

Annabeth slid off the couch and onto her knees, cushioned by the thick wool rug.

Dane obligingly sat up and spread his legs so that she could position herself between his knees. He reached for his belt buckle, and she swatted his hand away.

"Let me. You just sit back and think of England…or something."

He chuckled but obeyed her, letting his head rest against the back of the couch, spread out like a deliciously muscular banquet before her.

"Somehow, I don't think it'll be *England* I'm thinking of," he drawled.

"Not if I do this right," she agreed, her fingers busy with his belt and his zipper.

Dane obligingly lifted his hips and allowed her to pull down his briefs once she had his pants open. The rich rush of scent was intoxicating—clean male, a hint of sweat, the sharp musk of arousal, and something else. Something wild...

Annabeth licked her lips and leaned forward eagerly, putting her hands on his hard, muscled thighs. His newly freed cock was beautiful, thick and long, the head and shaft flushed and pulsing as it pressed tightly against his muscled belly.

Annabeth licked her lips at the sight and slid her fingers around his cock, enjoying the contrast between the soft, silky skin of his shaft and the hardness within as she pulled it forward.

She teased the sensitive head with her fingertips, and Dane groaned. It was a very gratifying sound.

"I want you," she said. "Inside me. Please, Dane."

"God, yes," he groaned.

With some effort, he extracted a condom packet from the pocket of his jeans.

"Let me," Annabeth said and plucked it from his fingers.

Annabeth took her time putting on the condom, unrolling it down his shaft with long, slow strokes, playing with him, teasing him.

Dane's breathing had turned rapid by the time she finished, and she found that her own arousal had returned in full, hot force.

She couldn't wait to climb on top of him, slide herself down on his erection, and feel him stretch her in wonderful ways as she rode him.

She glanced up and saw that he was watching her with predatory intensity, and she was acutely aware of her bared breasts.

"You are so beautiful," he breathed.

"So are you," she said sincerely and climbed back up onto his lap.

Every part of her ached to be filled by him. And she wanted to watch his face as she rode him to the finish line.

Then his cellphone rang, a harsh blaring ringtone that Annabeth recognized as the emergency summons.

"You've got to be kidding me," Dane groaned.

Annabeth wanted to scream in frustration as she scrambled off his lap. He leaned forward and dug for his phone in the jeans lying on the carpet.

"Shit, Annabeth, I'm so sorry," Dane panted. "Of all the bad timing—"

She shook her head, smiling wryly as he hit Answer.

"Dane here," he growled. "Yeah, I'm on my way—no, I'm just down the street. My turn-outs are in my truck. I'll be there in five."

He ended the call and struggled to his feet. With a grimace, he pulled the condom off his unrelieved erection before pulling on his jeans.

"Annabeth, I'm sorry. I have to go. It's a car accident—a bad one, sounds like."

"Hey, duty calls. I understand," she assured him, swallowing down bitter disappointment.

She'd been so close to having what might possibly have been the best sex of her life…

"Can I—do you mind if I come back after I finish the call?" Dane asked over his shoulder.

"I'd love that," Annabeth said. "Be safe, okay? And I'll see you later."

"Later," Dane said, making it sound like a promise.

Then he was gone, the apartment door slamming behind him.

Since she didn't know how long Dane's emergency call would take, Annabeth decided to leave the door unlocked, for once.

11

LOVED

Dane never returned that day.

Annabeth waited until it was past her usual bedtime, then crawled into bed, feeling bitterly disappointed.

She'd let herself hope that he'd be more than just a friend with benefits. She'd fallen for him, and hard.

But as she pulled the quilt over her, dark thoughts began to creep in. Why would a tall, gorgeous man like Dane want in her that way? She was only Fat Bethie, after all.

Annabeth had spent her entire life trying to prove that she was the nice, hardworking one while watching most of the attractive men she met go for the thin girls when they wanted to date someone.

Roger had been the first man who treated her like an attractive woman, but if his recent outburst was anything to go by, he had been lying to her all along.

And if Roger had been able to fool her like that, then how could she trust her instincts about Dane?

As Annabeth curled miserably under her quilt, she began to worry that something she had done or said on their date had given Dane second thoughts, and that was why he hadn't returned.

Her horrible, awful, no good day had ended on such an unexpected high note…and had shown her what kind of place Bearpaw Ridge was. Kayla, Fred Barker, Dane…she had friends here who were willing to help her out.

And she realized that this was what she had wanted all along…a place to belong.

Although she had only been here for a short time, Annabeth had never experienced anything like the sense of community she had experienced in this small town. People valued her here, and they were willing to help her out when she was in trouble.

They treated her like she mattered. Like she was *important*. Her mother had never done that; nor had Roger.

With them, Annabeth had always felt the need to justify her existence. *Don't cause a fuss, don't be a burden, always work hard so that they'll want to keep you around.*

Only Maggie had been different. And Maggie had come to the Bay Area from Bearpaw Ridge. That couldn't be a coincidence, could it?

Remembering everything that had happened that day, both good and bad, Annabeth felt a sickening clench of doubt. What if she couldn't make a profit with her bakery? What if tomorrow proved to be another series of disasters? What if she lost everything?

I'll have to return to the Bay Area. To Roger, she thought.

Her stomach roiled at the thought, and she felt sick.

I can't go back. I've outgrown the old Annabeth. Whatever happens now, I'm a different person. And I want to stay here, no matter what it takes.

Even if Dane's changed his mind about me.

When her alarm woke her early the next morning, she saw that Dane had sent her a text around midnight.

At hospital in Salmon. Accident was neighbor's son. Am staying until parents arrive. So sorry, I'll make it up to you tonight. I promise.

Annabeth stared at her phone and felt a weight lift from her heart. Last night's doubts and worries suddenly seemed far away. Of course, Dane wouldn't just abandon her. But he was a firefighter, and he had to go help whoever needed him.

And she was okay with that. In fact, it was one of the things she really liked about him.

She took a quick shower and got dressed in a clean pair of pants and chef's coat—bright magenta today.

Clutching a steaming mug filled with the sweet nectar of wakefulness, she made her way downstairs to the bakery to start the first batch of sweet yeast dough for cinnamon rolls.

Annabeth heard the front doorbell tinkle promptly at 4:45 a.m. and smiled. "Kayla, is that you?" she called.

"Good morning, Annabeth," Kayla's cheerful voice replied. "Do you want me get the coffee going?"

"That sounds great! Let me just put this batch of lemon bars in the oven, and then I'll come and show you the ropes," Annabeth replied.

The rest of the day passed quickly.

Kayla proved to be cheerful, hardworking, and on a first-name basis with nearly all of Annabeth's customers.

She rang up purchases, ran the espresso machine, and served the pastries while Annabeth remained mostly in the back of the bakery, mixing dough and rolling out the next batches of the cinnamon rolls.

Thanks to her new help, she even had time to make croissants and a batch of jam-filled Danish, using the delicious, locally produced apricot and huckleberry jams she had bought from the Ursus Acres farm stall at the local farmers' market.

Kayla turned out to be a skilled barista, which she played off with a shy smile and an offhand comment about having worked her way through college at a café near campus.

Undeterred by yesterday's unexpected closure, the bakery's customers were lined up out the door even before opening time, and business remained brisk until after lunchtime.

Annabeth was relieved to see them. She had been worried that the appearance of a restaurant inspector and the bakery's subsequent closure might have frightened people away.

After lunch, things quieted down, and Annabeth finally had a chance to chat a bit with her new employee.

She learned that Kayla had graduated from college in December with a bachelor's degree in biology and had been accepted at the College of Veterinary Medicine at Washington State University for the fall semester.

In turn, she told Kayla about working for Maggie at Cacao in San Francisco, carefully omitting any mention of Roger.

"Thank you so much for all your hard work yesterday and today," Annabeth told her new assistant with real gratitude as Kayla untied her spotless apron at 2:00 p.m. and hung it on a coat hook embedded in the wall just behind the register. "I'll see you tomorrow morning."

"Sure thing!" Kayla called, pushing open the bakery's front door with a cheery tinkle of the bell. "This job is fun!"

Things were quiet in the bakery for the rest of the afternoon, with occasional customers dropping by for coffee or to pick up something for an afternoon snack. With satisfaction, Annabeth noted that almost everything had been sold, and there would only be a few croissants and a dozen cookies to bag up at closing time and put in the "Day Old Discount" box.

Diane Felsbach dropped by late in the afternoon, not to inspect, but to purchase the last few lemon bars and huckleberry tarts.

"For my husband and kids," she told Annabeth with a wide smile. "I always try to bring back a treat if I'm gone overnight from home. And everything looked so yummy when I was here yesterday in my official capacity."

"I imagine you have a pretty big territory to cover," Annabeth said as she put Diane's purchases in a takeout box.

"I do, but I like to think that I'm doing important work." Diane paid, then extended her hand to Annabeth. "And I wish you the best of luck with your new business, Annabeth. I hope to see you next year."

Annabeth shook the restaurant inspector's hand. "I hope so too. Thanks for everything, Diane."

She was sweeping up the flour and crumbs when her doorbell tinkled once more.

"Hey, Annabeth!" called Dane's deep voice, and her heart soared.

She put aside her broom and hurried to the front of the bakery.

Dane looked tired after his long night at the hospital, but he was smiling and holding a pizza box in one hand and a six-pack of beer in the other, the dark brown bottles covered with condensation.

The pizza was from The Bear's Lair Pizza & Pasta restaurant across the street, and it smelled delicious.

Annabeth's stomach growled loudly, and she felt abruptly ravenous. She had been so busy today that she'd forgotten to eat lunch.

"I thought I'd drop by with dinner, if you still want to see me," Dane said, looking as if he really expected her to kick him out.

"Dane, you have no idea how happy I am to see you," she said, smiling at him. "Or your pizza. Give me a few minutes to finish cleaning up here, and then we can go upstairs."

"Take all the time you need," he said, dropping into one of the café's chairs. "I'm off-duty, and I'm not going anywhere."

"Good," Annabeth said.

He came back! He wants to spend time with me!

Sitting at the breakfast bar in Annabeth's apartment, they wolfed down the pizza and two of the bottles of Bearpaw Dark Ale, a smooth local microbrew.

"How did today go?" Dane asked around mouthfuls.

"Great! And Kayla was a big help. I can't thank you enough!" Annabeth said enthusiastically.

It had been a good day, and now it was ending on an even better note, with Dane sitting next to her, their shoulders touching occasionally as they ate.

Dane's tired features creased into a smile. "I'm glad."

Reminded of the reason for his weariness, she asked, "And what about the accident last night? Is your neighbor's son going to be okay?"

Dane sighed and rolled his shoulders. "Eventually. Josh has a couple of major surgeries ahead of him. It looks like he took a turn too fast. Rolled his car down an eight-foot embankment and landed on his roof in Steve Fraser's alfalfa field. Luckily, Josh was wearing his seatbelt, but he still got pretty banged up. Broken bones, heavy bruising, concussion. His car was a beater with no airbags."

"That sounds awful," Annabeth said. "I'm so sorry."

Dane finished off the last slice of pizza and sighed with repletion.

"It could have been worse," he said quietly. "A *lot* worse."

Annabeth studied his somber expression and wondered what kinds of "worse" things he had seen as a firefighter.

From what she'd overheard from Dane and his brothers whenever they stopped by the bakery, a lot of their emergency calls involved either car accidents or boating and swimming accidents on the river.

Then Dane seemed to shake off his gloomy thoughts. "I didn't bring dessert," he said apologetically.

Annabeth raised her brows and pouted.

"And here I thought *you* were the dessert," she said daringly.

Her heart pounded as she waited for his reaction to her outrageously flirty remark. She was going to feel really stupid if he turned her down.

Instead, she got a slow, hot smile.

"I could be," he said. "If that's what you want."

Annabeth swallowed, her throat feeling dry. "Yeah, I definitely want."

His smile widened, and he hopped off the bar stool. He reached for his shirt buttons. "Best news I've had all day," he said.

She reached out and caught his hands. "Let me."

Dane's eyes widened. He obediently let his hands drop back down to his sides.

Annabeth opened the top button of his shirt with tantalizing slowness and worked her way down, revealing hard muscle as the fabric parted. His chest was as broad as she remembered, his torso sculpted in ways that made her want to run her hands all over his taut skin.

She finished opening his shirt and pushed it off his shoulders.

"Wow," she said, admiring his biceps.

His arms looked as massive as tree trunks. No wonder he'd been able to move the Hobart without effort!

"*Wow* is good," he observed happily, "though I did start to feel hopeful when you didn't immediately slam the door in my face after I had to cut our date short last night."

"Dane, if I was the one in a car accident," she said, keeping her tone light despite a stab of guilt because she *had* been angry and hurt, at least for a little while, "I'd want to know that you and the other firefighters were responding as quickly as you could."

"I'm glad you understand," he said. "If something had happened to Josh because I couldn't make it there quickly enough, I'd feel really bad. His parents' ranch is a fair distance away—when the Medevac helicopter arrived, I went with him, so that he wouldn't be alone in the ER until his folks arrived. I knew it would be at least two hours before his folks could make it to the hospital in Salmon."

"I understand, really I do," she said, pressing her palm lightly against one hard, warm pectoral. "However, I'll cop to feeling really disappointed because you had to leave so suddenly."

"But you're giving me a second chance now, and that's all that matters," Dane said, suddenly serious.

"You made an excellent first impression, Mr. Swanson," Annabeth teased. "As it stands, I'm going to have to think of a way to return the favor tonight."

"I can't wait to see what you come up with," Dane whispered, his eyes half-closed as she yielded to the temptation and stroked his abs.

"Ooh, pressure." She ran her hand back up over his chest, enjoying the contrast between the springy hair and the firm muscle beneath. She had noticed before that his skin felt very warm to the touch.

"Lucky for you," she whispered, standing on tiptoes to lick his ear, "I've always performed well under pressure."

Letting her fingers skim lightly over his nipples, which hardened instantly, she slowly walked around him, still touching him. She explored his shoulders, his tautly muscled back, and his long, straight spine. She let her hands learn the shape of him and the texture of his skin.

"You're making a good start," he said, his breath coming faster.

Annabeth completed her circuit and stood before him once more. Her hands dropped to his waist. She touched his belt buckle. "May I?"

"I'm yours," he said simply, and she saw his pulse beating wildly in the hollow at the base of his throat. "Do whatever you want with me, Annabeth."

"Is this the part where I pull out my whips and chains?" she joked as she fumbled with his belt, then unbuttoned and unzipped his pants.

"Whatever the lady wants, I'm game," Dane said instantly. The bulge in his briefs supported his claim.

"Well, what I want right now is to see you naked," Annabeth said, hooking her thumbs under the waistband of his briefs.

She pushed them down, letting them fall to his ankles.

"Your wish is my command." Dane sounded a little breathless as he toed off his shoes and socks and stepped out of the crumpled heap of his jeans and underwear.

Then he stood completely still, letting her admire his long, muscled legs and beautiful firm ass.

His cock was completely erect, rising rigidly from the dark hair at his groin. It pressed against his belly, thick and flushed.

"Damn," Annabeth breathed in admiration. "You are one fine specimen of manhood."

He chuckled, and the movement of his diaphragm did nice things to his abs. "I'll try not to let it go to my head."

Annabeth stepped close and pressed herself against Dane, devouring his mouth. His canine teeth felt oddly sharp as she caressed them with her tongue.

He groaned, and his arms closed around her with painful strength as he returned the kiss, his tongue thrusting into her mouth as he pushed his hips against her.

She felt his erection hard against her belly, pressing through her clothes, and she wanted to wrap her legs around his waist and take him inside her *now*. Her pussy felt swollen and ached with the slow throb of arousal.

She shifted her mouth down to Dane's throat, kissing and biting at the rough, warm skin, feeling the faint prickle of incipient stubble against her lips.

He tasted delicious, and he seemed to enjoy it when she was a little rough with him, if his soft moans were any indication.

"Don't stop now," Dane panted when she finally drew back.

Then she saw the marks she had left on him, dark red and round against the side of his neck. Oh God, she'd actually given him a set of *hickeys!* What was she, in high school?

"I am *so* sorry. I don't know what came over me," she babbled, touching the marks as if she could smooth them away.

"No apologies needed," Dane said, pulling her back into his embrace. "I liked that. Do it some more."

"But—" Annabeth began to protest.

She wanted to mark him, to make sure everyone who saw him knew he belonged to her, but the primal urge frightened her.

"Please," said Dane, his tone less a plea than an order. He tilted his head back, exposing his throat in invitation.

"Oh God," Annabeth groaned.

But she couldn't resist the invitation, though she made sure to keep her urges more in check as she nibbled her way down his throat to his collarbones, feeling the strong beat of his pulse against her lips.

Dane's breath hitched and his pulse pounded furiously as Annabeth worked her way down his chest. His gasp was extremely gratifying when she took one of his nipples into her mouth and worked it mercilessly with her lips and tongue, just as he had done to her last night.

Then she bit him with carefully calculated pressure, and he moaned, sending a jolt of pure pleasure to her groin.

"I want you," she said hoarsely. "Now, Dane. Please."

"Oh gods, yes," replied Dane. He knelt and rummaged in the pile of his crumpled clothing, coming up with a condom packet between his fingers.

She quickly pulled her chef's coat over her head and felt his fingers at her waist, unfastening her pants.

A few moments later, she was standing before him in her everyday plain cotton underwear. Nothing sexy, but at least it was clean.

Dane didn't seem to mind. He was looking at her like a starving man. "I've been tasting you on my lips all day, Annabeth, and I want more."

"So do I," she managed, her mouth dry.

He smoothed his big hands over her breasts before tracing her bra straps around to the clasp in back and deftly unfastening it.

"The teddy bear undies are a nice touch," he murmured.

"Hey, I don't wear my lacy underwear all the time," she protested, sure he was being sarcastic. "But if you don't like them, feel free to take them off me."

She grinned herself as he did just that, with gratifying speed.

"I'm pretty fond of teddy bears," he assured her as he drew her down to the couch. "I just like you better without them."

Annabeth eagerly straddled his legs and took his cock in her hand. It was large and very hard, and she couldn't wait to feel him inside her.

She unrolled the condom quickly over his length and guided him between her legs.

The broad tip of his cock pushed into her, and she gasped. He was big. And it felt *glorious* as he stretched her wet, deliciously swollen entrance in a welcome invasion that she'd been fantasizing about since he first kissed her.

Dane's hands tightened on her hips when he was just barely inside her, and he stopped moving.

"Okay?" he asked softly.

She smiled down at him.

"Better than okay. You feel so—" Annabeth gave a happy sigh and wriggled a little, trying to encourage him to slide in all the way. "Great."

His hands slid up from her hips to her breasts as she rocked gently on him, each movement taking more of him inside her. His thumbs circled her nipples, teasing them with bright sparks of sensation as he thrust firmly upwards into her.

When he was all the way inside her, she arched her back, enjoying the feeling of being impaled on his hard length.

Dane kissed her breasts.

"Turnaround is fair play," he said, just before he drew her nipple into his mouth, sucking hard until she moaned from the pleasure, then biting down.

Her knees tightened around his hips as she writhed against him, panting.

"I'm going to fuck you now," he murmured, moving to her other breast and dropping light kisses on it as her nipple tightened with anticipation.

"Oh yes, please…"

And then he did, his hands moving back to her hips as he lifted her, letting his cock slide partway out of her, then surged up powerfully to fill her again.

She cried out with pleasure, her fingers digging into the thick muscle of his shoulders as she responded to his movements, riding him.

She caressed every part of him she could reach, running her fingers through his soft hair, tracing the curve of his ears, stroking the nape of his neck as she knelt astride his lap. Her thigh muscles flexed as she rose and fell on his cock, meeting each of his thrusts with her own.

His tongue and teeth continued to work her breasts until both of her nipples were stiff and swollen with his attentions. Dane moved powerfully against her, each wet stroke of his cock sliding against her clit, winding her up to climax.

He seemed to know exactly what she needed, because his movements suddenly became shorter and faster, and the coil of pleasure rapidly tightened in Annabeth's belly.

She clutched at him as she fell over the edge, convulsing with a surge of pleasure that made her inner muscles squeeze him in a rippling hold. Annabeth had never felt anything like this before, an orgasm that went on and on and seemed to come from her core in powerful waves.

When it finally died away, it left her satisfied but hungry for more.

She sat on his lap, shaking a little with the intensity of what she had just experienced. And realized that Dane was still hard and still inside her.

"Ready for more?" he asked hoarsely.

Annabeth nodded.

"Let's change position."

He lifted her with that amazing strength of his. Moments later, Annabeth found herself on her back on the couch, her legs draped over Dane's forearms as he knelt between her legs and spread her wide.

He dipped his head to her breasts, and just the lightest flick of his tongue against her sensitized nipples made her whimper and arch her back before he entered her again with one powerful thrust.

In contrast to their slow and gentle start, Dane took her hard and fast this time. She loved every second as he held her wide open and his hips moved in a merciless rhythm between her spread legs, driving her to another climax as he pounded into her.

This time, he came too, and she held him as he shuddered and gasped against her.

But he wasn't done yet.

After a session of making out that served to renew his erection while he stoked the fire in her belly, he put on a fresh condom and bent her over the padded arm of her couch, her legs spread apart and her forearms braced against the seat cushions.

He kissed his way down the length of her spine, then knelt behind her, licking and teasing every inch of her pussy with his tongue until she was writhing with need.

"Oh, God, Dane, please," Annabeth whimpered, teetering on the brink of another orgasm. "Please fuck me again."

"Your wish is my command." She couldn't see his face as he stopped his delicious torture and rose to his feet.

Then she felt him slide his thumbs into her entrance and open her wide for his cock.

He felt bigger from this angle, as he pushed into her and began to fuck her with long, slow, powerful strokes.

Her orgasm built gradually this time and broke over her like a long wave. She shook and sobbed with the pleasure of it, feeling her inner muscles ripple and squeeze him.

Then Dane scooped her up in his arms and carried her effortlessly over to her bed. His skin felt burning hot now as he cradled her against his chest.

He kissed her, slowly and lovingly, and she found he wasn't done yet, as she felt his still-hard cock pressing eagerly against her.

"One more time?" he asked softly as he put her down on her bed.

"Please," she said.

He made slow love to her with his hands and mouth, exploring her with tender kisses and touches, finding all of the secret places that made her shiver with pleasure—a spot on her neck, just behind her ear; the tender skin on the inside of her elbow, the dimples at the base of her spine.

After Dane's earlier treatment, Annabeth's breasts were still exquisitely sensitive. He teased them with the tip of his tongue and the pads of his fingers until she was panting and ready to come just from his caresses.

"I love how you respond to me," he said, kissing the soft curve of her stomach. "I've dreamed about doing this with you, Annabeth, but the real thing is so much better." His tongue dipped into her belly button, and she giggled.

He was dreaming about me? It seemed too good to be true…but then, she could hardly believe he was here with her, in her bed, doing sweetly dirty things to her while she begged for more.

"I'm glad I wasn't the only one having those kind of dreams," she said.

"This is a thousand times better than any dream." He moved lower and blew a teasing puff of air against her pussy. She opened her legs eagerly to him. "You taste so sweet, and I love to hear you enjoying yourself."

"Mmm, yes, you're really good at this," Annabeth said. Desire made it difficult to think, as she tried to come up with something that wouldn't sound completely lame.

He looked up and gave her a sweet smile that made her heart feel like it was melting.

Then Dane lowered his head between her legs and began to do things to her with his hot, wet mouth that left her unable to say anything coherent for a long time.

When she was teetering on the brink of coming again, she grabbed his head and pulled him up. "I want you inside me," she gasped.

He obeyed, covering her with his hard, heavy body as she wrapped her legs around his hips and clung to him.

With powerful strokes, he drove her to another orgasm before he came with a loud growl, his face buried in her cloud of hair, his breath hot against her cheek.

Afterwards, she felt completely satisfied but sore. Dane drew her quilt up over both of them. He spooned her, curling his hot body around her limp, exhausted form.

"May I stay the night?" he asked, cupping her breast as if he couldn't get enough of touching her.

"I'd really like that," she said. "If you don't mind my alarm going off at oh-dark-thirty. I'll make you coffee before I head downstairs to work."

"Sounds great," he said, his breath tickling her ear.

Feeling happier and more relaxed than she had in years, Annabeth fell asleep with Dane's arms around her and his broad chest against her back.

Dane was nearly asleep, basking in the afterglow of good sex and relishing the feeling of Annabeth cuddled against him, when the phone rang.

Annabeth started awake and flung out her arm, fumbling for the cordless phone on her nightstand.

"Hello?" she mumbled.

"Annabeth, why won't you talk to me?" demanded a voice that Dane's keen hearing instantly identified as her ex-boyfriend.

Dane felt her tense. Without a word, she disconnected and slammed the phone back onto its cradle.

"Sorry," she mumbled, curling back against Dane's side. "I don't know how he got this number. It's unlisted."

The phone began to ring again. Annabeth made an unhappy sound, and Dane clenched his jaw, trying to suppress an irritated growl.

The ringing stopped as voicemail picked up. Five seconds later, the phone began to ring again. The call went to voicemail. A short pause, then the ringing started.

Annabeth grew tenser and tenser with every repetition of the cycle.

"Why won't he just leave me alone?" she whispered.

"Because he's an asshole," Dane said bluntly.

His fingertips itched with the need to shapeshift into a grizzly's long, curving claws.

Dane the bear wanted to rip Roger's face off with one powerful swipe of his paw. And so did Dane the man, actually.

That desire grew as the phone continued to ring, and ring, and ring, and Annabeth grew stiffer and tenser in Dane's arms, unhappiness radiating from her.

Dane didn't like that. She'd been smiling and limp with his very thorough pleasuring when she dozed off. He had found deep satisfaction that he'd been able to do that for her.

And now...this *asshole* was making his mate unhappy. Dane couldn't just lie here and let it happen.

The next time the phone rang, Dane snatched the receiver over Annabeth's hissed protest and hit the Talk button.

"Is this Roger?" he demanded, hearing a growl shredding the edges of his words.

A shocked inhalation on the other end of the line, followed by a few moments of silence.

"Who is this?" demanded a voice that Dane recognized as Roger. "What are you doing at Annabeth's place?"

"I want you to stop calling this number. You're harassing my girlfriend, and I won't stand for it," growled Dane. "I know where you live, asshole. Don't make me cross state lines to come get you."

Another silence, broken only by the faint sound of the other man's breathing. Then the line disconnected abruptly.

Dane gave a small, satisfied grin as he replaced the phone on its charger.

He was willing to bet that Roger would chicken out on calling Annabeth's apartment again. Guys like that usually backed down at the first sign of real trouble. They were only willing to bully the people they thought wouldn't—or couldn't—fight back.

"And once again, my knight in shining armor rides to the rescue," Annabeth mumbled.

Dane couldn't tell whether she was joking or serious—she seemed so grateful for the smallest, most insignificant things, and it pissed him off to think how she'd been treated up until now.

"I think *rescue* is in my job description," he said wryly. "At least you don't need the Jaws of Life or a Medevac helicopter."

She rolled over to face him, an oddly intense look on her face.

"What is it?" he asked.

"Um, when you called me your girlfriend just now," she said shyly. "That was just to get Roger to stop calling me, right?"

Dane blinked at her. What? Of *course* she was his—

Oh, wait, we haven't talked about this part yet, have we?

But after what they had just shared, his bear wasn't going to stand for any other man staking a claim on her.

He only hoped he could get her to agree to be exclusive.

"Nope." Trying to appear confident and casual, Dane settled down in the bed, and gathered her soft, sweet-smelling body back into his arms. "I mean, I was hoping that…"

No, damn it, this is coming out all wrong!

He took a deep breath. "Annabeth, will you be mine? Beat off your horde of suitors and date only me?"

She stiffened against him, and for a panicked instant, he thought he'd said something wrong.

"Are—are you sure? *Me* as your girlfriend?" Why in hell did she sound so disbelieving? That asshole Roger must have really done a number on her!

"Yeah, you," he drawled. "The prettiest woman in Bearpaw Ridge…and the best baker, that's for damned sure."

"But—" she began to protest.

"Hey, why did you think all those guys are *really* lining up every morning?" Dane kissed her, enjoying the feeling of her bare skin and luscious breasts pressing against him. Desire stirred, and he didn't think he could ever get enough of her. "I mean, your cinnamon rolls are wonderful, but then there's *you*, with your sweet smile and those killer curves. So yeah, I'll consider myself the luckiest man in Lemhi County if you say you'll be mine."

"I—I don't know what to say," Annabeth sounded dazed, and not just from his kiss, as pleasant as that had been.

"How about *yes?*" suggested Dane hopefully.

Annabeth giggled. "Yes. Of course! But only if you're sure…"

He kissed her again. "I'm sure," he said. "I've been sure since the moment I laid eyes on you, Annabeth."

"Oh." It was her turn to kiss him now.

The feeling of her soft lips nibbling on him made him want to roll her on her back and make love to her again.

"Go back to sleep," he said, reluctantly, when she finally drew back and cushioned her head on his shoulder. "I know you have an early start."

She yawned and hugged him with the arm she had thrown over his torso.

"You make me really happy, Dane," she murmured and let her eyes drift shut.

Dane lay awake for a while longer, thinking.

His inner bear's restlessness had stilled for the first time in weeks, content now that they had made love to their mate.

But Dane found that the man and the bear were still at war.

How could someone so wrong for him feel, smell, and taste so right?

Annabeth was everything he'd ever wanted in a woman—kind, funny, and sweetly curvy in a way that had made him want to tear her clothes off and carry her to his bed the first time he saw her.

But she wasn't a shifter. Worse yet, she didn't know about shifters. Didn't know that most of the people in Bearpaw Ridge were shifters.

Now that he had laid his claim on his fated mate and she had accepted him, Dane knew he had to tell her, and sooner rather than later. And hope to God she could accept him, *all* of him.

Just not tonight.

Tonight, he wanted to savor the sensation of lying in bed with his mate in the sweet afterglow of their lovemaking, enjoying her wonderful scent and the touch of her bare skin against his, his mouth filled with the sweet, tangy taste of her pleasure.

Ours, rumbled his bear silently. *Forever.*

But Dane wasn't so sure. He remembered the last time he had had anything close to this. And how his final memory of Tanya was the shocked, betrayed, *terrified* expression on her face.

She had run out of the house right after he revealed himself to her. His heart had broken with the sound of her car door slamming as she peeled away.

He had finally gathered the courage to tell her the truth about what he was, despite his mother's dire warnings, and she had rejected him and run away.

Would Annabeth run, too? Dane wondered. Would she think he was a monster and leave him, like Tanya had?

He turned his head and gazed down at Annabeth's face, peaceful in sleep.

When she knew the truth about what he was, would she still trust him enough to fall asleep against him like this, relaxed and utterly vulnerable?

12

SECRETIVE

The next day was a very good day, with Kayla staffing the front of the bakery and the prospect of dinner with Dane to brighten the end of the day.

Annabeth found herself humming as she worked, and she realized that she couldn't remember ever being this happy.

She had sore muscles and tender spots to remind her about how amazing the sex had been last night…tender and fierce, gentle and hard by turns.

And she couldn't get over Dane, her amazing new *boyfriend*, and the way he acted as if he was grateful for *her*, rather than making her feel like she had to prove that she deserved him.

It was hard to get her head around this new relationship dynamic, but she liked it.

The hours flew by. When afternoon rolled around and the steady flow of customers dried to an occasional visitor, Annabeth and Kayla started on the end-of-day chores to clean up and prep everything for the following morning.

Emerging from the storeroom, Annabeth saw Kayla casually lifting the Hobart and moving it aside to sweep behind it.

She stopped dead and stared at her assistant.

Kayla was a big, athletic-looking girl, but still, the Hobart probably weighed three or four times what she did.

Is everyone in Bearpaw Ridge freakishly strong?

Annabeth waited until Kayla had gently lowered the Hobart back to the bakery's tiled floor before she said, "Please put that back when you're done cleaning, or I'll bump into it every time I need something from the storeroom."

Kayla jumped and whirled around, a guilty expression on her face. Her face turned bright red.

"Let me guess, Dane has you wrestling calves in your spare time?" Annabeth asked, still trying to process what she had just seen.

Kayla stared at her blankly for a moment.

"Uh, what exactly has he told you about our family?" she finally asked, her tone wary.

Annabeth blinked, surprised both by Kayla's reaction and by her question.

"Not too much," she admitted. "I know he's got four brothers who are all firefighters like him, that his dad passed away a few years ago, and that he's managing the family ranch."

"Oh." Kayla seemed disappointed.

Annabeth frowned and put her hands on her hips. "Kayla, what's going on? What's the big secret?"

Kayla looked suddenly stricken. "I can't tell you!" she blurted out. "You'll have to ask Dane."

"All right," Annabeth said, using her most soothing tones while she wondered what the hell was going on.

She'd noticed a few odd things here and there since arriving in Bearpaw Ridge, but she had mostly just ignored them, because they didn't seem like a big deal…just a little weird.

Then a terrible thought ambushed her.

"Just tell me—is it bad news?" She swallowed down nausea as conviction mushroomed. She had never been to the ranch, never seen Dane's house. And she only had his cell number, not his landline… "Dane—he isn't married, is he?"

"What?" Kayla exclaimed, looking shocked. "Of course not! Dane would *never* cheat on his ma—uh, girlfriend."

A rush of relief made Annabeth feel dizzy. "Good," she breathed.

She continued, "And he's not a serial killer or anything?"

Kayla giggled, looking equally relieved. "Nope."

Annabeth considered this. "Well, then, I guess I can wait for him to confess all," she said.

"I wish he would," Kayla said fervently. "There's some stuff—not illegal, or anything," she added hastily at Annabeth's raised brows, "but important stuff he needs to tell you. And we're all getting tired of tiptoeing around it."

"What on earth—" Annabeth began, but Kayla shook her head.

"Just ask Dane. Please."

As it turned out, Annabeth didn't see Dane that evening or for the next three days.

Lightning sparked the first big wildfire of the season in the dry Bureau of Land Management, or BLM, lands that lay east of town. The Bearpaw Ridge Fire Department's crew of volunteer firefighters were called out to assist the BLM wildland firefighters.

Dane texted Annabeth to apologize for canceling their dinner date, which was nice of him but unnecessary, since Annabeth and everyone else in town could see the huge clouds of smoke billowing from the ridge on the other side of the valley.

That ridge and the rest of the spectacular mountain views quickly disappeared from view behind a sullen brown haze that closed in around Bearpaw Ridge as the hours passed.

The afternoon sun turned a shade of twilight orange, an effect Annabeth had experienced during similar wildfires in California, which shrouded the Bay Area in smoke every couple of years.

Fred Barker's wife Linda came around about an hour before the bakery closed, asking for donations to feed the firefighters.

She was a dark-haired woman in her late forties, with vivid blue eyes and a sweet smile.

"My youngest two—they're twins—just got their drivers' licenses," she explained. "Emma and Sophie are planning to drive up to the staging area first thing tomorrow morning and deliver breakfast and boxed lunches. The Bear's Lair Pizza and Pasta delivered lunch and dinner today—lasagna, spaghetti, garlic bread, and salad. The Brown Bear Market is donating sandwich fixings and fruit for tomorrow's lunch, and the Bearpaw Brewing Company is donating cases of bottled water and sodas. The Bear-B-Q Pit will be sending up spareribs and pulled pork with all the fixings for tomorrow's dinner, but we need something for breakfast."

Annabeth thought of Dane, Evan, Mark, Fred, and all the other firefighters she had come to know over the past few weeks.

"I can supply breakfast pastries and snacks," she offered. "I could make a batch of turnovers filled with scrambled egg, ham, and cheese, plus cinnamon rolls and Danishes. Brownies, lemon bars, and cookies for snacks. And I'll have my two big coffee urns ready to go. What time would you need everything ready for pickup, and for how many?"

"There are about sixty firefighters up on the ridge right now, including our boys, the BLM crews, and volunteers from the Salmon and Challis Fire Departments. If you're willing and able to provide for that many, that would be wonderful," Linda said with a breathtaking smile. "Especially the coffee and cinnamon rolls. I imagine that Fred and the others will be working all night to try and control the fire. I'll send girls around at 6:00 a.m."

Annabeth nodded. "I'll have everything ready to go by then," she promised.

She poured a cup of coffee and offered it to Linda, who was probably facing a sleepless night herself. "Have you heard any news? Is everyone okay?"

Linda accepted the coffee with a grateful smile and shook her head. "Not since they went out of cell range. It's a big fire, but as long as the wind keeps blowing from the west, we should be okay." Annabeth saw the other woman take a deep breath. "And no was transported to the hospital in Salmon during my shift as emergency dispatcher, so I'm hoping that means no one's been hurt."

"I hope so, too," breathed Annabeth, trying not to think about Dane—or his brothers—surrounded by burning trees.

He's not alone out there. He's got the rest of the BPRFD and the BLM crews with him.

But she still worried.

Kayla and Annabeth kept the bakery closed for the first part of the following morning. With most of the Bearpaw Ridge FD out in the field, there were only a few early birds to disappoint.

While Annabeth made the breakfast pastries, both sweet and savory, that she had promised Linda, Kayla brewed gallons of coffee and packed up the food along with disposable insulated cups, sugar, creamer, and stir-sticks to accompany the huge insulated urns of coffee.

Normally the coffee would be brewed on-site, but Kayla had told her that the firefighters' base camp probably wouldn't be equipped with power outlets or reliable running water, so they had decided to prepare everything ahead of time and hope for the best.

When Fred's twin daughters turned up promptly at six, both teenaged girls slender and blonde and fragile-looking, Annabeth nervously eyed the big urns, which were filled to the brim with hot coffee.

"Do you need a hand—" Annabeth began, just as Emma lifted one of the big coffee urns from the counter as if it weighed nothing.

"I'm okay," Emma assured Annabeth in a breezy tone as she easily gathered up the second urn in her other arm.

Annabeth gaped at the display of raw strength. Was this what growing up in the mountains did for people?

She had bought those two urns to use if she was ever asked to cater an event. They were at least four times the size of the Airpot thermal carafes she used for her daily operations, and when filled, weighed at least sixty pounds each, if not more.

Sophie, equally fragile-looking, lifted the entire stack of bakery boxes, each box filled with pastries.

"Maybe you could open the door for us?" she suggested cheerfully. "Thanks a million, Annabeth. I know how much Dad likes your cinnamon rolls."

Don't stare. Act normal, Annabeth told herself.

"If you see Dane, will you tell him 'Hi' from me?" Annabeth asked, holding open the bakery's front door as Emma and Sophie passed by with their burdens.

A large red pickup was parked in front of the bakery, its truck bed already filled with shrink-wrapped flats of bottled water and cans of soda as well as big cardboard boxes filled to the brim with boxed lunches.

"We will!" Sophie assured Annabeth as she helped her sister hook bungee cords around the coffee urns to keep them upright and in place as they drove up what would probably be a fairly bumpy dirt road to the staging area.

"Wait a sec," Annabeth said. "I almost forgot—I wasn't sure if you two had a chance to grab any breakfast yet, so I made a couple of extra ham-and-cheese turnovers for you."

"Yum! Thank you!" the twins chorused, as Annabeth ducked back inside the bakery and hastily wrapped up the breakfast pastries in waxed paper for them.

Stay safe, Dane. Please, Annabeth thought as the laden pickup truck pulled away from the curb and headed out of town.

Like everyone else in Bearpaw Ridge, Annabeth kept an eye on the wind over the next few days, praying it wouldn't shift and drive the fire towards people's homes and businesses.

She and Kayla continued to open the bakery two hours later than usual, using the first few hours of the morning to prepare coffee and breakfast for delivery to the firefighters.

Emma and Sophie came by twice a day, in the mornings to pick up the food and coffee, then returning around dinnertime to deliver the empty coffee urns for cleaning and refilling. They also brought updates about the progress of the firefighting efforts and let Annabeth know that they'd seen Dane, but he had been working and was too busy to do more than say a quick "Hi."

Still, even that little bit of news helped loosen the knot of anxiety in Annabeth's stomach. Dane was safe. That was all that mattered.

The fire was officially controlled on the morning of the fourth day, and exhausted firefighters slowly began trickling into town around lunchtime as their teams were demobilized.

When news of the demobilization reached them, Kayla helped Annabeth decorate several of the tables in the café area with streamers and a couple of plastic firefighters' hats scavenged from Halloween costumes. They bought poster board and made a big sign to hang in the café's front window:

Thank you BPRFD and BLM Firefighters! Free coffee and pastries!!

Throughout the afternoon, the bakery hosted a steady stream of tired, grimy men and women dressed in firefighters' turnout gear, and Kayla was kept busy serving them with complimentary pastries and drinks.

Annabeth tried to concentrate on her work, but she was waiting anxiously for her phone to ring.

Fred Barker and his sons stopped by briefly to apologize for the delay in starting the rewiring job and to assure her that now that the fire was contained, they would begin working on the bakery later in the week.

She saw other volunteer Bearpaw Ridge firefighters that she knew, but no sign of Dane or his brothers.

When she heard the tinkle of the bakery's doorbell in the late afternoon, and the sound of familiar male voices, she abandoned the mixer she was cleaning out and dashed to the front of the bakery even before she heard Kayla call for her.

"Dane!" She felt a rush of relief at the sight of his tired, stubbled face.

He looked up at her voice and opened his arms wide while Mark and Evan grinned at her.

She flew into his embrace and kissed him thoroughly, to the sound of approving whistles.

Dane was dressed in bunker pants and a sweat-stained navy blue T-shirt with "Property of Bearpaw Ridge FD" written across the chest in white lettering. He smelled of smoke and dust layered over sweat, and she was overjoyed to see him.

"I'm glad you're okay," she whispered. "I missed you."

His big arms tightened around her. "Missed you, too, sweetheart. I'm dying for a cup of coffee, and then I have to go home to take care of a few things, but I want to come back and have dinner with you. Is that okay?"

"More than okay. I'm just glad you're back," she assured him.

That got her another long kiss, deliciously needy and spiced with the scrape of stubble against her lips and cheeks.

When he finally released her, her heart was pounding, and the place between her legs was throbbing with need. And there were still several hours to go before dinnertime…

Evan sighed. "Ah, young love. So sweet," he said sarcastically.

Annabeth's cheeks grew hot, but she stayed where she was and just smiled at Dane's younger brother. "Be nice, or I'm going to run out of pastries before I get to you. Too bad, so sad."

Evan clapped his hand over his heart and staggered dramatically backwards, as if he'd been punched, while Mark and Dane both laughed.

Annabeth noticed that Evan was wearing a jester's hat, the velvet points limp and grimy and festooned with jingle bells.

"Nice hat," she commented.

Dane chuckled.

"Tell her what it is," he urged Evan, who rolled his eyes and shook his head, making the bells ring.

Mark said, "It's the Departmental Fool Award, presented to any BPRFD firefighter who does a spectacularly dumb thing while out on a call."

"Oh?" Annabeth raised her brows in Evan's direction. "And what did you do to win the award?"

Evan's face was suddenly looking flushed under the layer of dirt.

"All right, all right," he said, putting up his hands. "I was a dumbass, okay? I left the tanker truck in neutral when we, uh, exited the vehicle—"

"—which wouldn't have been so bad, except he also forgot to set the parking brake," interjected a grinning Mark.

"—I heard yelling when I started walking over to the staging area," Evan continued, glumly. "I turned around just in time to see the tanker rolling backwards down the hill."

"And it didn't stop until it T-boned a state trooper's car parked about a quarter-mile down the road," finished Dane, dropping into one of the café's chairs with a weary sigh. "Luckily, the officer wasn't in his car at the time."

Mark shook his head with fake sympathy as he seated himself next to Dane. "Our little brother was so excited about fighting a real fire that he completely forgot how to park a vehicle. Luckily for him—and us—there's only minor damage to the tanker. The cop car…well, that's another story."

"Well, I'm glad no one was hurt," Annabeth said, trying not to laugh at Evan's woebegone expression under the jester's hat.

Inspiration struck her. "Wait here—I have a special treat for you, Evan."

"Wait just a minute there," Dane hollered after her in mock indignation as she rounded the counter and headed for the back of the bakery. "How come *he* gets a treat for messing up?"

Mark added, "Yeah, do you know how much paperwork we're going to have to fill out tomorrow because of him?"

Annabeth smiled to herself as she grabbed a couple of piping bags and quickly filled them with some leftover frosting from the cupcakes she had baked earlier. *Now, I just need to add a bit of food coloring to this one…*

"Here you go, Evan," she said a few minutes later.

Dane and Mark roared with laughter when they saw the clown cupcake she placed in front of Evan. Their laughter was joined by that of the BLM crew seated at the next table.

As Annabeth headed back towards the counter with the intention of fetching her boyfriend and his brothers a generous pile of the lemon bars they liked so much, she overheard an enigmatic snatch of conversation directed at Dane.

"What do you mean you haven't told her yet?" Mark demanded in a loud whisper.

Evan added, "You gotta tell her, Dane. Especially since she's your—"

"Not here!" Dane growled, and Evan stopped talking.

Out of the corner of her eye, Annabeth saw Dane's shoulder's slump.

He added, sounding defeated. "I'll tell her. I just…need a little time."

She remembered her conversation with Kayla a few days ago and shook her head. *What on earth is going on here?*

She decided that although she was dying to find out what Dane was supposed to tell her, she could wait until he was ready to talk. Even if the suspense killed her in the meanwhile.

At least I know Dane's not married or cheating on me, Annabeth tried to reassure herself. *Whatever his big secret is, it can't really be that bad, can it?*

13

REUNITED

After the bakery had closed for the day, Annabeth headed upstairs to her apartment to shower, change out of her work clothes, and wait for Dane to arrive.

As she passed her mailbox at the base of the stairs, she noticed a small padded manila envelope sticking out.

It was very light and had a printed label with no return address.

She took it upstairs with her. Once inside her apartment, she opened it with a great deal of curiosity.

A Ziploc baggie slid out into her palm, and Annabeth stared down in disbelief. It was the pearl-and-sapphire pendant on a gold chain that Roger had given her for her birthday last year.

She had been overwhelmed by his generosity…until he confiscated it just before Christmas, to punish her when she had failed to get a discount he wanted on their existing satellite TV package.

The Ziploc bag was jittering in her hands, and she realized that her hands were shaking.

She saw a piece of folded paper tucked into the Ziploc bag and pulled it out. It looked like it had come from the notepad that sat next to the landline in Roger's condo.

Her gut roiling with anxiety, she unfolded it and immediately recognized his writing.

Come home, Bethie. This has gone on long enough. You can stop punishing me now. I get it, okay? I need you, and I don't care if you were dating that guy who answered the phone. Just dump him and come home. All my love, Roger

With a chill, Annabeth realized that not only had Roger somehow unearthed her unlisted phone number, but he had found her address as well.

Probably through some Internet people-finder site, she thought numbly.

She rose from her couch and shoved the baggie into the top drawer of her chest of drawers. She couldn't tell Dane about this. He'd insist on confronting Roger, and she was afraid it might get ugly.

Roger would be no match physically for Dane, but if Dane took a swing at her ex—and she knew he would—Roger wouldn't hesitate to try to get Dane arrested for assault. Or maybe worse.

Dane was really, freakishly strong. He might kill Roger by mistake. The thought made an icy chill run down Annabeth's spine.

No, she *definitely* couldn't tell Dane about this.

Besides, she didn't think Roger would actually come here to make trouble for her.

For one thing, he was always so busy at work that she couldn't imagine that he could find the time for a road trip to the middle of nowhere. Bearpaw Ridge was a fourteen-hour drive from the Bay Area and at least a two-hour drive from the nearest major airport.

But hearing from him had certainly managed to put a damper on her reunion with Dane.

Or so she thought, until Dane actually showed up, showered and shaved…and carrying a big bunch of pink and yellow roses which looked like they had come from his garden rather than from a florist.

He handed her the roses, which smelled wonderful, then kissed her until she was warm all over and shaking with need.

"Oh God, Dane, you have to stop now, or we'll never get around to eating dinner," she pleaded, breathlessly, when they finally parted.

He inhaled deeply and made a point of glancing between her and the kitchen, as if trying to decide between the two of them.

She had left an elk stew simmering in her crockpot all day, using meat that Kayla had given to her. Annabeth had decided to cook the unfamiliar meat like a Boeuf Bourguignon, with bacon, onions, garlic, herbs, mushrooms, vegetables, and lots of red wine.

To round out the meal, Annabeth had brought up a fresh, crusty baguette from the bakery and some leftover apple turnovers. She had to admit that her apartment smelled pretty damned good right now.

"Woman, you've presented me with an impossible choice," he declared. "Food or you—how can I possibly decide?"

"You can have both," she informed him, reluctantly extricating herself from his embrace and heading for the kitchen. "Just not at the same time."

He groaned but didn't protest when she lifted the lid from the crockpot and began ladling out the stew into a pair of bowls.

His first bowl disappeared while she was serving herself.

Annabeth tasted the stew, decided she really liked it, and poured a glass of Cabernet for each of them. She had used about half the bottle in the stew and thought this was a nice way to finish off the other half of the bottle.

As she ate, she enjoyed the sight of Dane wolfing down her food. He had seconds, then thirds, also demolishing most of the baguette in the process.

Finally he sat back with satisfied sigh.

"That was outstanding," he told her, wiping his mouth with his napkin and downing the last swallow of wine.

"I've got dessert. Should I make some coffee?"

He shook his head and rose, circling the table to stand behind her.

"The kind of dessert I want doesn't go well with coffee," he informed her, lifting her hair to kiss the nape of the neck.

She shivered with the pleasant jolt of sensation, then let him draw her up into his arms for another long, deep kiss, flavored with wine and herbs this time.

"I missed you," he whispered, drawing back just far enough to speak. His lips brushed her skin with every word, and his warm breath mingled with hers. "I thought about you a lot while I was up on the ridge."

"I missed you, too," Annabeth said, and a wave of desire caught her, robbing her of breath.

God, she wanted him! Wanted to taste every inch of him. Wanted to feel him *everywhere*.

She put her hands on his hips and sank slowly to her knees before him.

"Dane?" she asked. "Can I—?"

"God, yes. Please," Dane answered, his voice rough with desire.

She licked her lips as she ran her hands up his hard, muscled thighs. She eagerly unbuttoned the waistband of his jeans and carefully pulled down the zipper. Dane was already half hard.

Eagerly, she pulled down his briefs and used his own trick, blowing gently on his cock to tease him.

He smelled wonderful, soap and musk and his own special scent.

Dane groaned softly, and the sound went straight through her in a rush of welcome heat.

She pushed up his shirt, slid her hands around to his tight ass and pressed her breasts against his thighs while kissing the hard planes of his stomach and belly.

She felt every muscle in his body tense. She felt his cock move against her, as if he'd just gotten harder.

Annabeth leaned back, curled her fingers around his shaft, and felt him twitch under her touch as she stroked him with lingering movements until he was fully erect, while she enjoyed the contrast between the soft, silky skin covering his cock and the hardness within as she pulled it gently forward.

She teased the sensitive head with her breath and the tip of her tongue and heard Dane's breath hitch as she tasted salt.

This is going to be a lot of fun, she realized.

Roger had always wanted blow jobs from her, so she'd gotten good at giving them, but they had never been her favorite thing.

Until now. She couldn't wait to drive Dane crazy with her mouth. She wanted to give him as much pleasure as he'd given her last time, and she knew she would enjoy every minute of it.

She glanced up through her lashes and saw that Dane was watching her with predatory intensity in his hazel eyes.

"That feels amazing," he murmured.

"And I'm just getting started," she promised him.

Then she opened her mouth as wide as she could and engulfed him. He reacted with a gratifying gasp.

While she worked him with her mouth, she continued to caress his shaft with firm strokes while her other hand toyed with his sac.

"God, Annabeth, that feels so good," he said, his voice uneven as his breath caught and hitched. "It's been a long time since someone did this for me."

"Mmm," she said.

She felt him shiver at the vibrations of her voice.

His hands came to rest on her head as she worked on him. She felt his fingers slide into her hair, caressing it.

She liked feeling the subtle shifts in his muscles as she touched him and relished hearing the changes in his breathing when she did something that he liked.

After a blissful interval, she felt his thigh muscles tighten.

"Annabeth, stop," he said raggedly. "I want to come inside you."

A little reluctantly, she pulled away.

And almost instantly found herself on her back on the rug, his hands at her waist, pushing up her summer dress and yanking off her panties. She discovered that she loved being manhandled like this, liked how he was in complete control now.

He paused to put on a condom before parting her legs with his big callused hands and covering her with his hard, heavy body.

Annabeth wrapped her legs around his hips as he entered her with a powerful thrust.

Pleasuring him had turned her on, too, and Dane felt so good inside her. It was thrilling to be stretched out like this on her living room floor, both of them still half-dressed, as he devoured her mouth and rode her hard and fast.

Her climax took her by surprise, the pleasure sweeping over her in an unexpected wave. An instant later, she felt Dane's stomach muscles tense. He convulsed, driving his cock deep into her welcoming flesh with short, sharp jerks as he rode out his climax.

He was still hard inside her when he sighed and relaxed, his hands gentling on her hair. "I can't get enough of you," he murmured.

"Does that mean you're ready for another course of dessert?" Smiling up at him, she rose shakily to her feet, took his hand, and led him over to her bed.

It was paradise to be naked in Annabeth's bed, skin to skin with her, her lips and hands and body touching him everywhere.

Every kiss, hot against his skin, every firm caress, every sigh of pleasure melted Dane's brain as he and Annabeth made love with slow tenderness.

He had missed her these past few days, consumed with yearning for her in the midst of the endless slog of fighting a wildfire, the heat and smoke and sheer exhausting hard work of it, interspersed by occasional moments of adrenaline-pumping terror when the wind shifted and the flames came roaring in their direction.

Truth be told, he was a little embarrassed about throwing her down on the floor and fucking her like that, but the feeling of her hot, wet mouth on his cock had made his bear take control. It had claimed their mate in the only way it knew how.

And she had enjoyed it as much as he had, apparently. God, what a woman!

Dane didn't think he'd ever stop wanting her. She was his mate, the only woman for him, now or in the future.

Yielding to his need to feel her heat, inside and out, once again, he rolled them both over, pinning her beneath him on the soft mattress. She arched up eagerly to meet him. Her arms and legs were wrapped around him and her hot, wet core pressed eagerly against him, surrounding him in a tight grip as he slid into her once more.

Shaking, he kissed her long and deep as he sheathed himself fully inside her.

Now that Annabeth had yielded to him, he *belonged* to her.

But was she strong enough to give him what he needed?

He wouldn't know until he revealed himself to her—and the prospect terrified him. Annabeth had been raised in a world where shapeshifters and magic were the stuff of movies and novels.

Once she knew what he really was, would she want to bind herself to him?

But she was *his*. And he was hers, and the truth of that could not be denied as he moved against her with long, deep thrusts.

He made love to her with every bit of skill he had, using everything he had learned about her during the past few weeks.

Just as she touched, stroked, nibbled, kissed, and caressed every inch of him, he did the same to her, needing to hear her soft gasps and her whimpers as he brought her to the edge again and again.

And when she climaxed, he drowned in the sheer bliss of hearing her sob out his name, her pleasure summoning his own release.

Dane made love to Annabeth until they were both satisfied at last, and she lay panting in his arms.

He pulled her quilt over them both, and Annabeth wrapped herself around him, cuddling close.

Even then, sated as he was, he couldn't keep from kissing her delicious lips. And she responded to him with the same eagerness she had shown when he had first arrived.

"So I was wondering," Dane murmured, and felt Annabeth's arm tighten around his waist. "Do you have any plans for tomorrow night? Would you like to come to the ranch for Sunday dinner and meet my mom? My brothers will be there, too."

Annabeth tensed, and he wondered if he was moving too fast.

"I'd love to," she said.

14

ENGAGED

"Damn, Dane, I haven't seen you this nervous since senior prom," teased Mark as he watched Dane pacing around the ranch house's living room.

Dane scowled at his brother, tried to stand still, and found himself pacing again a few seconds later.

He could hear his mother setting the table in the dining room, and the house was filled with delicious smells of roasting prime rib and baking potatoes.

Mom had reacted with a mixture of worry and excitement when she heard that he had invited Annabeth to dinner. Worry because Annabeth wasn't a shifter, and excitement because he hadn't introduced her to any of the few-and-far-between women he'd dated since Tanya.

At least Mom now seemed to be resigned to the fact that Dane and his bear had found their fated mate in an Ordinary human woman.

He peered anxiously out of the living room window and saw a cloud of dust in the distance. Annabeth was coming!

The road from the highway to the ranch house was unpaved, but it had been graded just a few weeks ago, so he didn't think her little Prius would have any problems making it up to the house.

"You know we all really like her, right?" Mark said, his tone serious now. "I was a little worried when I heard she'd come all the way from California, but she really seems to fit in here." He paused, and Dane felt his brother's keen scrutiny. Mark's voice dropped to a conspiratorial whisper. "You still haven't told her about being a bear shifter, have you?"

"What?" said Mom, poking her head into the living room as her keen shifter ears overheard the question. "What do you mean she doesn't know? And your bear has *mated* her? Dane, what on earth!"

Dane turned to look out the window again. It was preferable to seeing Mom's disappointed expression.

"I know," he said with resignation.

"You can't really blame him," Mark said, quick as always to defend his big brother. "After what happened the last time, I mean."

Mom just sighed and shook her head before heading back to the kitchen.

Dane swallowed down a lump of guilt. He knew he was way past the point where keeping a secret like this from Annabeth was a good idea, but somehow, he hadn't been able to bring himself to tell her last night.

She had been so generous, so hungry for him. He couldn't stand the thought of seeing her warmth and affection turn to fear and loathing.

But he had to tell her. And soon.

Dane watched as the dust cloud drew closer and closer until finally the little blue hatchback pulled up in front of the house. It was dwarfed by the two large Ford pickups already parked there. The old pickup was used for work around the ranch, and the new one was used for running errands in town. Both were emblazoned with the Grizzly Creek Ranch logo.

When the Prius driver's side door swung open, Dane immediately went to the front of the house and opened the door.

"Hey there, beautiful," he said, smiling as Annabeth approached, walking up the short flagstone path between the flowerbeds of lavender, cosmos, and other summer blooms.

She looked radiant in a light turquoise summer dress, her glorious red-gold hair loose around her shoulders. He bent to kiss her lips, which shone with tinted lip gloss and tasted of black cherry.

"Careful!" she said in mild alarm as he put his arms around her, and it was then he noticed that she was carrying a bakery box.

He felt a presence behind him and turned to see Mom.

"You must be Annabeth," Mom said warmly, extending her hand. "I'm Elle. I'm so glad to finally meet you. Everyone has been talking about how wonderful your bakery is."

Color tinted Annabeth's smooth cheeks. "That's really nice of them. I'm really glad to meet you too," she replied. "I, uh, brought dessert. I hope you don't mind," she added, and Dane froze.

He should have told her not to bring anything. Mom prided herself in providing everything a guest might want or need, and for Annabeth to bring food to Sunday night dinner might be taken as an implied criticism…

He braced himself for—well, he wasn't sure what.

But Mom only smiled warmly and accepted the proffered box. "Why, thank you! That's very thoughtful of you, and I can't wait to serve it."

Dane's mother was very nice, Annabeth decided as he led her inside the beautiful Victorian ranch house. She had been nervous about meeting Elle and really wanted to make a good impression.

So far, so good.

The front door had a semicircular antique stained glass panel set above the doorframe, and a wide wooden staircase curved in a crescent up to the second story. The wall of the foyer was covered with framed photographs ranging from Victorian daguerreotypes in silvery grays and blacks to more recent color photos.

"Our family has owned this ranch since 1870," Elle said proudly when Annabeth slowed down to look at the photos. "We were among the first settlers in the area."

The matriarch of the Swanson family was a tall woman with frosted blonde hair and hazel eyes and an air of good-natured common sense. Annabeth had liked her at first sight.

Elle pointed at a more recent photo, which showed a handsome, broad-shouldered man who looked like an older version of Dane, sitting on a patch of grass under a tree with four little dark-haired boys clustered around him. "And that's Dane on his tenth birthday, with his brothers and his late father."

"I'm sorry for your loss," Annabeth said.

Elle smiled sadly. "I still miss him, but Dane and his brothers really keep things running smoothly around here these days."

"Only because you do most of the paperwork," Dane protested. "And that's the hardest part."

Elle glanced at Annabeth and answered her unasked question. "It was a car accident. We think the other driver either fell asleep at the wheel or had some kind of medical event like a heart attack or stroke. No way to tell, afterwards—it was a head-on collision, and both cars were nearly destroyed."

"Oh, that's awful," Annabeth said, responding to the old pain coloring Elle's voice.

On impulse, she leaned forward and gave Elle a hug, which the other woman returned.

When they drew apart, Elle smiled at her. "I'm so glad Dane invited you to join us here tonight. And I think dinner is nearly ready, if you'd like to come along."

Dinner was served in the formal dining room with its antique wallpaper and molded plaster ceilings. The food was delicious, a prime rib from the ranch's cattle that melted in Annabeth's mouth, served with crisp seasoned oven fries and steamed snap peas fresh from the ranch's vegetable garden.

To Annabeth's surprise, she and Elle were the only women seated at the big mahogany table. She had already met all of Dane's brothers, except for Thor, who lived in Denver and usually only visited home a few times a year.

She liked them and was pretty sure they liked her, too, if their good-natured teasing at the bakery was anything to go by.

"Dane tells me you moved here from San Francisco," Elle said to Annabeth, amidst the busy clinking of silverware against plates as the brothers ate with gusto. "What made you decide to come all the way out here?"

"My boss at Cacao Cakes—that's where I worked when I still lived in California—was Maggie Ornelas," Annabeth replied, trying to decide whether she should mention Roger, or not.

She glanced around the table at the four big men and decided *not*.

"Well, some personal stuff happened, and I decided to make a fresh start. Maggie told me that someone in her hometown was retiring and that he had listed his bakery for sale at a really good price. I decided that it was the opportunity of a lifetime and took the plunge."

"The Ornelas family are good people," Elle said. "I remember Maggie from when she was a little girl. And we all like Manny—he's done a lot for the town."

"He was the first person I met in Bearpaw Ridge, and he's been really nice and really helpful," Annabeth said.

"So you're planning to stay in Bearpaw Ridge, then?" Elle asked.

Her tone was casual, but Annabeth saw her gaze flick sideways to Dane, who was seated next to Annabeth.

The subtext was clear: *Are you planning to leave my boy? Are you going to break his heart?*

Annabeth nodded, eager to reassure Elle—and Dane, too, if he was worried.

"I really like it here," she said. "And the bakery is doing pretty well so far. Everyone I've met so far has been incredibly nice, and I've never lived in a place where no one locked their houses or their cars." She added, feeling shy, "I haven't broken the habit of locking up yet, but I hope to one day."

Elle's smile this time was pure relief. "I'm glad to hear that, Annabeth. I've lived here all my life, except for the four years when I was away at university in Seattle. Back then, I couldn't wait to come home again."

Ashton, Dane's youngest brother, who was long, lanky, and eighteen and the owner of a successful video game startup that he ran out of his house on the ranch, grinned at Annabeth. "I was wondering why you locked your car when you arrived just now."

Annabeth felt her face grow hot as she realized how that might look like she didn't trust the Swansons.

"Force of habit," she explained, feeling self-conscious. "I don't even remember doing it."

"Not," Ashton said, as he served himself a second helping of the prime rib, "that it would stop any of us from getting into your car if we really wanted to. All we'd have to do is tear the door off. Grrr!" He made a swiping motion, like a grizzly bear hooking a salmon.

"Ash!" Dane said, angrily, as Annabeth stared at Ashton, trying to figure out if he was serious. "*Not* funny."

"Ashton," said Elle in a Mom Voice.

Ashton winced under the weight of Elle's stern look and flushed.

"Sorry," he mumbled. "I forgot. I, uh, was only joking. I wouldn't wreck your car, Annabeth. Honest!"

But Annabeth couldn't help but remember how easily both Dane and Kayla had been able to lift her huge Hobart floor mixer.

Maybe the Swanson family are X-men or something, she thought. *That would explain a lot of things about them.*

"I spoke to Dr. Bolton, and he says we can start administering the blackleg vaccine to the calves next week," Dane said into the awkward silence.

Following Dane's cue, the dinner conversation turned to ranching topics, which Annabeth found interesting if completely alien. All of the Swansons answered her questions cheerfully enough, though, and the rest of the meal passed pleasantly.

They finished eating, then cleared the dishes from the table in preparation for serving dessert.

Annabeth rose to help in the communal cleanup, carrying a stack of dishes through a set of swinging doors into the kitchen.

It was a big, old-fashioned room that took up most of the rear of the ranch house. It had been carefully modernized, keeping the original Victorian cabinetry and layout while updating with modern appliances. It smelled of brewing coffee now.

"This tart looks wonderful!" exclaimed Elle, carefully removing it from the box. She admired the jewel-like confection of glazed strawberries, raspberries, blueberries, and kiwifruit arranged on top of a layer of vanilla custard. "It's almost too pretty to cut."

"I hope you like it," Annabeth said. "And thank you so much for inviting me to dinner. It was delicious, and I really appreciate it."

Elle smiled warmly at her. "I hope you'll come again next Sunday," she said. "It's a ranch tradition that we all dine together on Sunday nights, no matter how busy the week has been."

"I'd really like that," Annabeth told her, feeling a warm glow in her chest at the invitation. She hoped that it meant that Dane's mother liked her. "Can I bring dessert again?"

"We still have an hour or so of daylight left. Would you be interested in a mini-tour of the ranch?" Dane asked, after Annabeth's tart had been reduced to a few crumbs and smears of berry juice.

"I'd love to," Annabeth said, to Dane's relief. She glanced down at her strappy sandals. "But I'm not sure I can do a lot of walking in these."

"No problem," Dane assured her, glad of a chance to get her alone. "We'll use one of the trucks. It's a little far for an after-dinner stroll, anyway."

"And there's a great place to view the sunset up on the hill," Mom added, sipping her coffee.

Dane was relieved that dinner had gone so well and that Mom seemed to have taken a liking to Annabeth. But he was going to kick Ash's butt later on for nearly spilling the family secret...

Keeping an eye on the sky and the sun's progress to the horizon, Dane drove Annabeth on a quick circuit of the ranch's main acreage.

They started at the hay and alfalfa fields in the rich bottomlands next to the river, then drove up into the drier sagebrush and grass-covered hills that comprised most of the ranch's lands. He pointed out the BLM lands on the forested heights of the mountains that framed the valley, and he explained that the Grizzly Creek Ranch had grazing allotments there, driving the cattle up into the higher altitudes to forage during the summer months and then rounding them up again in the autumn using ATVs and horses.

"So you guys *really* are cowboys," Annabeth exclaimed. "That's cool!"

Dane grinned at her. "I've even got the hat and boots to prove it," he teased. "If you ever want to learn to ride a horse, let me know."

As they bumped along the ranch's network of dirt roads, Dane occasionally slowed or stopped his truck to point out the local wildlife: a flock of sandhill cranes, tall and graceful, feeding in a pasture, and a small herd of pronghorn does bounding through the sagebrush, accompanied by their long-legged fawns.

Annabeth's delight in the sights warmed him. She might be a city girl, born and bred, but she genuinely seemed to love living here. *Good.*

He didn't want her to ever return to California. She belonged *here*, with him. He wanted her to love this land as much as he did.

Dane managed to make it to the top of the hill in time for a spectacular sunset, the brilliant oranges and deep cinnamon shades a lingering remnant of the wildfire that still smoldered nearby, though it was fully contained now and being carefully monitored by BLM.

"Wow," breathed Annabeth, her expression rapturous as she gazed through the windshield.

Dane had put his arm around her shoulders when he parked the truck, and she cuddled close to him.

"It's a nice view, isn't it?" he asked. "You can see nearly all of our ranch from up here." He took a breath. "Annabeth, when Mom asked you about your future plans earlier, I was really glad to hear that you're planning to stay in Bearpaw Ridge."

"I am. Like I told your mom, I really like it here. And I don't really miss California," she said, but added dryly, "though my opinion might change once I have to deal with snow."

Okay. This is where I tell her that the Swansons are bear shifters.

He took a deep breath and opened his mouth, preparing to confess.

But what emerged was, "I know we haven't known each other for very long, but...will you marry me?"

Annabeth turned her head to stare at him, her beautiful blue eyes wide with surprise. "You want to marry me? *Me?*" she said, her voice rising to a funny squeak.

"Yes, you. And only you," Dane said, his arm tightening around her shoulders. "I haven't been able to stop thinking about you since we met. And when we're together...it just feels *right*."

"It does," she agreed and reached to interlace her fingers through his.

"I want to be with you, Annabeth Jones. I want to share a bed with you every night, wake up with you every morning." He chuckled. "And since we both have to get up at God-awful hours, I want to have breakfast with you every day. And I want to see what our kids might look like."

Annabeth was silent, but she was squeezing his hand hard enough that his fingers were starting to go numb.

"I, uh, don't have a ring or anything, but if you say yes, I'll buy you a real nice one," he added, knowing he was babbling now.

She smiled and turned her head to kiss him. "It's crazy, but I've fallen head over heels in love with you." Then she sobered and raised her free hand to caress his cheek. "If I marry you, can I keep working at my bakery? Or would you expect me to move out to the ranch?"

"Of course you can stay at the bakery! Hell, the people in town would lynch me if they thought I was responsible for closing you down," he said, laughing.

He felt giddy with elation. *She's going to say yes!*

"I'll just move to town, and we'll rent a house or something. I can drive to the ranch—it's not like it's very far from town. I'll have to stay at the ranch full-time during calving and during the fall roundup, but that's only a few weeks out of the year. I'd be with you the rest of the time."

Annabeth smiled and kissed him again. She made it last a good, long, sweet time.

When she drew back, Dane saw her eyes were bright with unshed tears. "Yes, I'll marry you, Dane."

He whooped and gathered her up for another kiss. As he devoured her lips, his bear rumbled in silent approval at his success in securing their mate.

"I love you," said Dane. "Let's go back to the house and tell my family. I know they'll be thrilled."

As he drove back down the bumpy, twisting ridge road, Dane remembered that he still hadn't managed to tell Annabeth about being a bear shifter.

And now, more than ever, he knew he needed to.

Just not tonight.

He wanted to soak in this feeling of happy triumph for just a while longer, before his beautiful fiancée learned the whole truth about the Swanson clan…and the other shifters living in Bearpaw Ridge.

15

ENRAGED

"Oh, wow, that's great!" Kayla said, grinning, when Annabeth shared her news at work first thing the next morning. "Have you set a date yet?"

"Sort of," Annabeth replied.

After the dinner at the ranch and celebratory glasses of champagne all around, she and Dane had returned to her apartment, where he had spent the rest of the night making enthusiastic love to her.

When they parted before dawn, she had floated down the stairs to the bakery in a cloud of happiness.

She knew she should be having second thoughts about committing herself to a man she had met only a few weeks ago, but Dane was The One. She was absolutely sure of it.

And she couldn't wait to marry him. In between bouts of lovemaking last night, they had discussed the best time for their wedding.

"We're thinking about early September, maybe right after Labor Day weekend," Annabeth continued. "Dane says the weather is still generally sunny and warm for an outdoor wedding BBQ. The summer tourists will be gone, and things at the bakery will quiet down until hunting season starts. And we'll be able to take a short honeymoon before the autumn roundup of the ranch's cattle begins."

"I'm so excited for you! We've all been worried about Dane since Tanya—" Kayla stopped, apparently spotting Annabeth's confusion. "Wait, Dane hasn't talked to you about Tanya? Has he told you about, uh, *anything?*"

Tanya? Who the hell is Tanya? An ex? Dane had never mentioned her.

Annabeth shook her head. "I figured that as long as he wasn't married or wanted by the Feds, I'd just let him tell me on his schedule. But I have to admit," she added, "the mystery is starting to drive me crazy."

Kayla shook her head. "You're not the only one," she muttered. "Jeez, I'm going to smack Dane the next time I see him."

Annabeth laughed. "Don't damage my fiancé, okay? I've seen how strong you are."

Inspiration struck as she looked at her assistant, who was dressed in jeans and a tight pink T-shirt this morning, her hair pulled back in a ponytail. "Hey, Kayla, I don't know when you're planning to head off to vet school, but if you're still around in early September...would you like to be my bridesmaid? I'm going to call my mom and Maggie tonight with the news and ask Maggie if she'll be my maid of honor, but I'd really like to have you in the wedding as well."

"I'd love to," Kayla said instantly. "That'd be great! Oh, Annabeth, I'm so happy for you!"

And she gave Annabeth a bruising hug before Annabeth went to start rolling out the first batch of cinnamon rolls.

"And I'll tell Dane he needs to talk to you!" Kayla called after her, just before the coffee grinder roared to life.

The rest of day passed quickly. There was always a lot to do at the bakery, though Annabeth found herself staring off into space more than once, her current task temporarily forgotten as she made and discarded plans for her wedding.

Her *new* wedding.

Funny how she had almost forgotten that the date for her canceled wedding to Roger was only a week away. So much had happened in the past few weeks, and her life was so different now.

Uneasiness stirred at the thought of Roger and the sapphire pendant tucked away in a drawer upstairs.

Late in the afternoon, Annabeth heard the bell tinkle from the front of the bakery.

Kayla's shift had ended a while ago, and she had already gone home for the day, so Annabeth called, "Just a moment!" and washed her hands before she went to the front counter to help her customer.

She stopped dead when she reached the register and saw the tall blond man in the expensive suit standing there.

Shock traveled through her, and she felt like someone had flung a bucket of ice water over her. Her heart began to pound crazily.

"Hello, Bethie," the newcomer said with that lopsided smile that she had found attractive, once upon a time

Roger.

Roger had found her.

She hadn't gotten away from him after all.

Panicked, Annabeth looked around and noticed that there weren't any customers in the café area. She was on her own.

"What do you want?" she asked and was surprised to hear how calm her voice sounded.

"What do I *want?*" Roger asked, looking incredulous. "I want you to come home, Bethie. We're supposed to get married next week."

"What? We *broke up!* I moved to another state so that you'd get the message."

Annabeth took a deep breath. Her hands were shaking. Her knees were shaking. And her heart was pounding so hard that she was surprised Roger couldn't hear it.

His expression crumpled. "Bethie, don't do this to me! You have to come back!" She saw him swallow hard. "I know you've been mad at me, but I promise everything will be different from now on. Just—just come home. Please."

Annabeth shook her head. "No. I don't think that would be a good idea."

He looked like he was about to start crying. Annabeth quashed an automatic surge of guilt.

She wasn't responsible for his feelings, she told herself. Or the fact that he couldn't accept that their relationship was over.

"But *why?*" demanded Roger, his voice breaking. "I thought you loved me!"

"I thought I did, too. But I see now that it wasn't a healthy relationship." Annabeth's hands, out of sight behind the bakery's counter, were clenching the loose fabric of her chef's pants.

"Bethie...*please!*" he pleaded. "I need you!"

"No, you don't." Annabeth shook her head again. "I've made a new life here, and I'm not going anywhere."

She paused, trying to gauge Roger's mood. The awful feeling of walking on emotional eggshells was so familiar.

Funny how she'd never had to tiptoe around Dane like he was set to explode at any moment. It was one of the many reasons she loved him.

Roger sneered, his lip twisting. "How can you even stand it here? It's Hicksville Hell—all cowboys and country music, and the nearest Starbucks is *miles* away."

"Five hundred miles away, in Boise, to be exact," Annabeth said, forcing herself to smile pleasantly. "Which is why the café part of my bakery is doing really well. The only other café in the area is Sufficient Grounds, and it's in the next town over."

"You're actually *serious* about this?" Roger appeared utterly boggled. "You really *want* to stay…here?"

"Roger, go home," Annabeth said, trying for gentle-but-firm. "It's too late for us, but I'm sure you'll find someone else to date in the Bay Area."

Annabeth saw the instant that her words sparked Roger's anger. Rage flared in his eyes.

She took an involuntary step back.

"What about the anger management class I took? What about all the counseling I paid for? The deposit money on the Tea Gardens?" he demanded, his face twisting into an ugly snarl. "I did all those things *just for you* because I wanted to make you happy! I changed for you! You *owe* me!"

The old Annabeth would have cowered and apologized in the face of his anger. The new Annabeth felt an answering spark of annoyance.

And Roger hadn't changed one bit.

"If you did all those things, it should have been to help yourself," she snapped. "Not to try to manipulate me into getting back together with you!"

"And exactly what do you mean by that?" he demanded.

"I mean that I hope you'll take whatever you learned in that class and use it with your next girlfriend." *Gentle but firm*, she reminded herself. "And now I think you need to leave. Goodbye Roger."

His face darkened and she saw his fists clench. *Uh-oh*.

"You—you don't get to tell me to leave!" he sputtered. "Not after everything I've done for you!"

He was really scaring her now, but she knew she couldn't let him see that.

The old-fashioned landline phone on the wall behind seemed a million miles away—and who was she going to call, anyway?

The police? All Roger had done so far was *talk* to her, no matter how upsetting that was.

Dane? She knew her fiancé would charge over here in a heartbeat if he knew Roger was here and giving her trouble...but she didn't want to involve him and escalate the situation even further.

"Roger," Annabeth said, as sternly as she could, with her knees shaking. "Don't you get it? I am *done* with you. I moved all the way out here because I knew you'd go off the deep end if I tried to break up with you face-to-face."

As she spoke, Roger's face, already flushed under his expensive haircut, darkened until she thought he might have a stroke. His blue eyes bulged with rage.

"I'll show you *going off the deep end!*" he shouted.

Looking around wildly, he grabbed one of the chairs from the table behind him and raised it.

"Don't!" Annabeth shouted as Roger took aim at a glass display case filled with cookies.

If he broke it, the case would cost about $3000 to replace...a crippling expense.

Roger raised the chair to shoulder height, his face twisted with rage.

And the bakery's front door opened with an incongruously cheery tinkling sound as Dane pushed his way inside.

"Hey!" he growled. "What the hell do you think you're doing?"

Startled, Roger dropped the chair. It clattered loudly on the black-and-white marble floor tiles, making Annabeth jump.

Shaking, she put her hands on the counter to steady herself.

Thank God! Thank God it was the time of day when Dane and the other firefighters usually stopped by for coffee and whatever pastries were left over from the morning rush.

She saw Mark and Evan enter the bakery close on Dane's heels. All three brothers had apparently just returned from a call, because they were wearing their firefighting pants—*bunkers*, Dane called them—and BPRFD T-shirts.

They were also wearing matching scowls as they glared at Roger.

Annabeth saw Dane's nostrils flare as he inhaled deeply.

"You," he said, his voice still a deep, menacing growl. "You're Roger Pemberton, aren't you?"

Roger's eyes widened and he backed up a step.

"Thought so," Dane said with soft menace. "Get out."

Roger shot Annabeth a glance filled with anger and hurt and headed for the door.

Silently, Mark and Evan stepped aside to let him pass.

Roger put his hand on the door knob, then stopped and looked over his shoulder at Annabeth.

"I'm giving you until tomorrow to get your head on straight," he blustered. "Or you'll be sorry, you fat ugly bitch!"

Dane roared with primal rage. Moving with blinding speed, he pulled Roger away from the door and spun Annabeth's ex around to face him.

Annabeth gasped as she saw Dane grab Roger's upper arms and lift him effortlessly several inches off the floor.

"Let go of me!" Roger shouted. He looked scared now.

"Not until you apologize to Annabeth," Dane said, flatly.

Roger wriggled and kicked, to no effect. Annabeth could see that her ex wasn't going anywhere until Dane decided to let him go.

"I'll have you arrested for assault!" Roger yelled. "I'll sue you!"

Annabeth went cold. Roger would do it, too. She knew that about him. And he was rich enough to keep it up for a long time.

But Mark only laughed at the threat, and the sound boomed through the bakery.

"Good luck with that, Mr. Pemberton," he said. "I happen to be this town's lawyer, and if you're the same Roger Pemberton who's been harassing my future sister-in-law, then there isn't a law enforcement official in the county who'll arrest Dane if he decides to beat you to a pulp for threatening her."

"Yeah," added Evan, crossing his heavily muscled arms. "We all saw you holding that chair, looking like you were about to start swinging it, and poor Annabeth here—" he glanced over at her with exaggerated concern "—looking all scared out of her mind.

If Dane slugs you, then Mark, Annabeth, and I will tell the sheriff that he was just protecting her against an asshole out-of-towner who attacked her."

At his words, Annabeth drew a breath that caught in a sob of pure relief and gratitude. It humbled her to see that it wasn't just Dane defending her…it was all of the Swanson brothers.

"Just give me an excuse," Dane said quietly. "The only reason you're still alive right now is because you didn't actually touch her."

Annabeth's eyes began to sting, and her vision turned blurry.

I'm not going to cry, she told herself fiercely. *I'm not going to let Roger see me cry!*

"You can't do this to me!" Roger protested, sounding petulant now.

"You try to sue, and I'm betting the judge will laugh you out of court," Mark told Roger. "Now, get out of here before I decide that my client would best be served with a restraining order against you."

Roger struggled in Dane's iron grip, his feet kicking empty air.

"Dane," Mark said softly. "Let him go. I'm sure he's going to leave town now and never come back."

"Please, Dane," Annabeth said. "He didn't hurt me. He just yelled at me, that's all."

Dane growled softly, an almost inaudible rumble. His eyes had gone nearly gold. With obvious reluctance, he opened his hands and let Roger drop to the ground.

Roger landed on his feet with a thump and staggered before regaining his balance.

He headed for the door but was halted by Dane's hand landing on his shoulder.

"Oh no you don't. Not before you apologize."

"I'm sorry, okay?" Roger managed. "I shouldn't have done that. But you *made* me do it, Bethie! If you'd—"

"That's the sorriest excuse for an apology I've ever heard," interrupted Dane. "Get the hell out."

Roger glared at Annabeth, then slunk out of the bakery like a dog with his tail tucked between his legs.

All three Swanson brothers turned to watch him get into his silver BMW.

As Roger gunned his engine and roared away from the curb, Evan said in disgust, "What an asshole!"

Dane rounded the counter and took Annabeth in his embrace. She slid her arms around his waist and clung to him while she tried to get herself under control.

"I'm sorry we didn't get here sooner," he murmured. "Mark saw that car go by the firehouse, and we should have known something was up. I mean, who the hell drives a Beemer in Bearpaw Ridge?"

"Thank you," she said shakily. "I never thought he'd actually come here."

"No problem," Mark told her. "You're family now, Annabeth. Anyone who messes with you messes with us. *All* of us."

"Got that right," agreed Evan.

16

INCINERATED

Dane's phone woke them both up in the middle of the night, blaring with the strident ringtone used to summon the volunteer firefighters to an emergency.

Annabeth kissed him sleepily as he rolled out of bed.

She mumbled, "Be safe," before rolling over and sinking back into an exhausted sleep. She didn't even hear her apartment door close behind him.

Sometime later—she was never quite sure how long it was after Dane left her apartment—her smoke detector went off.

As she started awake out of a deep sleep laced with disturbing dreams about being chased through a dark forest by something menacing that she could hear but not see, she caught a faint whiff of smoke.

Then she heard the fainter sound of the bakery's fire alarm coming from the ground floor and the rush of water through the building's pipes as the sprinklers were triggered.

"Don't panic, don't panic, don't panic," she chanted under her breath as she scrambled up and grabbed for her clothes.

She dressed in haste, then looked wildly around her loft. What were the most important things she could carry with her?

She sprinted for the bookcase against the wall of her living room area, where her photo albums were stored. As she passed her coffee table, she grabbed the slim, silver laptop along with the thick manila folder containing her most important business paperwork.

Then she picked up her phone and dialed 911.

"911, what's your emergency?" asked a calm female voice. Before Annabeth could answer, the dispatcher asked, "Annabeth is that you, honey? What's going on? The bakery's alarms just went off. Are you okay?"

Annabeth recognized Linda Barker's voice, and somehow that helped. A weird sense of calm descended.

"Yes, but I think there's a fire downstairs. " she said, shouting to be heard over the strident sound of her smoke detector.

"Are you still in the building?" Linda asked.

"Yeah, but I'm heading for the door now..." Annabeth said, shifting her awkward burden of laptop, photo albums, and manila folder to the other arm.

"Okay, stay on the line with me, honey," said Linda. "Before you open the door, touch it and tell me whether it's warm or not."

Annabeth reached for the doorknob and found it hot to the touch. She knew that was a bad sign.

She looked down and saw a thin trail of smoke seeping under the metal door. "Dammit!"

"Annabeth, what's happening?" asked Linda.

"I think the fire is right outside my front door!" Annabeth said, her voice rising. "The handle is hot, and I can see smoke!"

"Okay, hon, I've notified the fire department. The boys are on their way, but it'll be a few minutes," Linda said. "Take a deep breath and look around. Can you wet down a kitchen towel and put it at the base of the door?"

"Y-yeah, I think so," Annabeth said and hurried to do so. It would help keep the smoke out of the loft for a while longer.

"Good," Linda said. "Now tell me about the windows. Can you open them and climb out?"

Right. Windows. There was no fire escape, and it was a pretty big drop to the sidewalk, but it probably wouldn't kill her. Probably.

Annabeth dumped her armful of albums and her computer on her bed and pushed up the large sliding window.

The century-old building that housed her bakery and apartment was made of brick. It was the middle building on the block, and the upper story only had windows along the facade overlooking Main Street. All the other natural light in the loft came from the skylights cut into the roof…at least 15 feet above her head.

She stuck her head out of the window and looked down. There were a few people gathered on the street below. She recognized most of them as her customers.

Someone waved at her. "You okay?" he shouted.

"Yeah," Annabeth called back. "Just trying to get out of here."

She leaned out further, looking for footholds in the brick façade of the old building.

Then, directly below her, the bakery's plate glass windows exploded outwards with a roar of flame and a great billowing cloud of smoke, cutting off her escape route.

"Annabeth? What's going on?" Linda asked.

Annabeth tried to keep the panic out of her voice as she answered. "I think I'm trapped."

The call that had kicked Dane out of Annabeth's bed had been for a solo rollover car accident on the highway just before the turn-off for the Bearpaw Springs Resort.

Dane, Mark, Evan, and Fred Barker were on call with the BPRFD this week, so they responded with a fire engine and a paramedic van. All of the town's volunteer firefighters were certified as EMTs, and Dane was driving the pumper truck, in case the car had caught on fire or there was gasoline spilled on the road.

The fire engine, with its bulk and flashing lights, would also help to control traffic on the highway by closing the lane and securing the scene while the firefighters did what they could to help the accident victims.

Problem was, when they reached the turnoff, they couldn't find the accident.

They drove slowly past the turnoff, each of them peering intently at the pastures and hayfields on either side of the highway, looking for any signs that a car gone off the road.

Nothing.

They continued up the highway, still looking.

After they had driven five miles past the reported scene of the accident and still hadn't spotted anything, Evan radioed Dispatch to verify the reported location.

In the rush to respond to an emergency call, it occasionally happened that firefighters incorrectly noted the location of an incident.

But Linda Barker, who was working Dispatch tonight, verified that the person who called in the accident had definitely said the Bearpaw Springs Resort turnoff.

So the little convoy found a place to turn around and headed back down the highway to the turnoff.

The mood was tense. Dane and the others knew that precious seconds were ticking by, with someone possibly badly injured or trapped in wreckage. And here they all were, driving around like tourists.

Still nothing.

They even drove up Bearpaw Springs Resort Road for several miles.

Were they missing something important? Or had the reported location been a mistake?

Dane hoped not.

Bad enough if they'd been hauled out of their beds in the middle of the night for nothing.

Worse yet if an accident *had* happened, and they were looking in the wrong place while someone in a wrecked car waited for help that never came.

"Damn it," Mark said, after they had made three more passes and still hadn't found anything. "You think this was someone's idea of a prank?"

Dane shook his head. "Who knows?" he said wearily. "It's happened before."

But usually on a Friday or Saturday night, when kids with too much beer in their systems thought it would be funny to see fire engines racing by on a mission to nowhere.

"I find out who did this, I'm gonna kick their ass," Evan said grumpily from the rear seat. "Even if we head back now, it'll be time for morning chores by the time I get back to the ranch." He yawned.

Dane radioed in the situation. He could hear Linda sigh. "Yeah, probably a false alarm. All right, have Fred make a couple more passes in the van, just to make sure. The rest of you can come back in."

They had just turned the engine around when the radio sprang to life again. "This is Dispatch," said Linda. "We're getting multiple reports of a fire on Main Street." She paused, and Dane felt a cold chill run down his spine. "And the alarms have gone off at the Cinnamon + Sugar Bakery."

Annabeth!

Dane accelerated as quickly as he could. Their ETA was at least 20 minutes back to town.

As he drove through the night, his initial chill of apprehension only spread at the thought that Annabeth might be in danger.

He recalled the rage in Roger's face at the bakery when he was shouting at Annabeth, who had gone white as a sheet but had bravely stood her ground.

Roger had wanted to hurt her then, Dane was sure of it. His keen bear nose could smell a killing rage, and Roger Pemberton had reeked of murderous intent.

Dane had been surprised when the man backed down so quickly after he and his brothers showed up.

At the time, he had thought it was because Roger was a coward who only dared to threaten a lone woman.

But now Dane wondered: was it a coincidence that the Bearpaw Ridge Fire Department had been called away on a false alarm at the same time that a fire broke out at Annabeth's bakery?

Not just her bakery. Her home. Where he had left her sleeping…and vulnerable.

Dane glanced over at Evan, who looked as tense as Dane felt, and pushed the engine to its limits.

17

EXPOSED

When they arrived, roaring up Main Street with the siren on and lights flashing, Dane saw with horror that Cinnamon + Sugar was engulfed in flames.

A group of off-duty firefighters had assembled, and someone had connected a hose to the nearest hydrant. They were fighting to contain the raging fire inside the bakery on the ground floor.

"Annabeth's trapped up there," shouted Avery Brooks, pointing at an open loft window, confirming what Dispatch had already told them on the drive into town.

Thick smoke was pouring out of the open window, and Dane prayed that they weren't too late.

"We went around back to try and get her, but the staircase was already burning," Avery continued. "We saw her at the window earlier, and then the fire downstairs rolled over and blew out the bakery's windows."

The next few minutes were a blur as Dane and Evan raised the engine's ladder to reach the open window twenty feet above.

Dane scrambled up the ladder in his bulky turnout gear, mask, SCBA tank, and helmet, his bear rising inside him at the danger to their mate.

Let her be all right, he prayed as he climbed rapidly, the weight of his gear nothing to his shifter strength.

Evan was right behind him.

"Annabeth!" Dane called as he climbed through the loft's window. He peered through the thick smoke for any sign of his mate.

He found her sprawled on the floor between her bed and the window, overcome by smoke. But alive, thank God.

Dane scooped her up in his arms just as Evan reached the window.

Dane pointed at the pile of albums and the laptop sitting amidst the rumpled bedclothes, and Evan nodded.

Afterwards, Dane didn't remember carrying Annabeth out of the loft and down the ladder, but then he was on the sidewalk, and Mark was there with his medic kit.

With an effort of will, Dane stepped back and let his brother examine Annabeth. Mark was a trained EMT and probably a lot calmer than Dane right now.

"I think she'll be all right," Mark said as he fitted an oxygen mask over Annabeth's face.

Dane saw her eyelids flutter and hoped to God that his brother was right. She was alive, and right now, that was all that mattered.

He pulled down his mask and turned to survey the scene, ready to join the firefighting efforts and save what was left of Annabeth's bakery and the apartment.

Then the breeze shifted, and Dane caught a whiff of a familiar scent mingled with the stink of smoke and chemicals. *That asshole Roger!*

He tracked the scent to the crowd of onlookers standing behind a hastily erected tape barrier at the end of the block.

Dane's gaze met Roger's, and he saw the other man's eyes widen in guilty terror.

Roger turned and ran.

And Dane knew then, without a doubt, that the fire that had almost killed Annabeth had been no accident.

Dane's bear, enraged beyond all measure, broke free. It was all Dane could do to strip out of his bulky—and expensive—turnout gear before the shift overwhelmed him.

When he rose in bear-shape a few moments later, he tore away the shredded remnants of his pants and T-shirt with a few irritated swipes of his paw.

Then he galloped in pursuit of his prey.

"You go, Dane!" someone shouted as the crowd of onlookers scattered to make way for him.

Even with his head start, Roger didn't stand a chance against a full-grown grizzly. In his bear shape, Dane could easily run 35 miles per hour, and he could keep up that pace for a long time.

The breeze brought Dane the scent of his prey, expensive cologne overlaid with the stink of gasoline and the rich perfume of terror. He stretched into an all-out run.

Away from the scene of the fire, the streets of Bearpaw Ridge were dark and deserted at this time of night.

Three blocks later, he caught up with Roger as the man was trying to climb into his BMW.

Dane roared in triumph at cornering his prey.

One furious swing of his paw ripped the car's door off its hinges and sent it skidding down the street with a spray of gravel.

Roger shrieked and hit the car's Start button.

The BMW's engine sprang to life with a throaty growl an instant before Dane hooked Roger's shirt with his curving claws and pulled the screaming man out of his car.

Roger landed on his back in the street. Sobbing with terror, he curled up into a fetal position, covering his head with hands. Lights began to come on in the homes all up and the street, and out of the corner of his eye, Dane saw curtains moving as residents peeked out.

But Bearpaw Ridge was a town populated by shifters, most of whom had no desire to come between an angry bear and its prey.

The sharp smell of human urine rose suddenly, and Dane huffed with ursine satisfaction at his prey's quivering terror.

He remembered what Annabeth had told him about her ex—the constant belittling, the emotional abuse, and those fucking *lists*.

And the taint of smoke clinging to Roger's clothing reminded Dane of the terror he had felt when he had seen the ground floor of the bakery building engulfed in flames.

Roger Pemberton didn't deserve to live. No, he was going to die very painfully for what he'd done to Annabeth.

Then flashing blue lights caught Dane's attention.

He swung his head around to see the sheriff's car pull up and park behind the BMW.

He gave a deep warning growl as Bill Jacobsen climbed out of his vehicle.

"Shoot it!" screamed Roger, uncurling suddenly from his fetal position. "For God's sake, shoot it! Shoot the bear! What are you waiting for? It's gonna *eat* me!"

With Dane momentarily distracted by the sheriff's arrival, Roger tried to scramble away.

Almost casually, Dane reached out a huge forepaw and pinned him in place. *You're not getting away that easily, you asshole.*

"Now, Dane, you caught him, fair and square," the sheriff said in soothing tone.

The bear rumbled agreement. *Mine!*

A wolf shifter himself, Bill had been serving Bearpaw Ridge for twenty years, and he was well-versed in handling shifters in their human or animal forms.

His hands spread out before him, Bill approached Dane with slow, cautious steps.

"But I can't let you kill him," he told Dane. "No matter how badly he deserves it."

Dane snarled. He *wanted* to kill Roger, wanted to see the asshole's blood soaking into the gravel of the street.

"If you kill him, I'll have to arrest you. And then you won't be able to look after Annabeth while she's in the hospital," Bill continued, his tone still calm. "So why don't you let me have this guy? I'll arrest him for suspected arson—"

"Why the fuck are you talking to a bear?" Roger screamed. "Just fucking *shoot* it before it eats me!"

"You stink of gasoline, and we have witnesses who saw you hanging around the bakery just before the fire started," Bill told him. "And when I search your car in a minute, I'm betting I'm going to find all kinds of interesting things to support my theory."

Roger squirmed frantically, trying to wriggle out from under the giant paw holding him captive.

Dane applied a bit of pressure to stop him and felt Roger's ribcage flex beneath his paw. He was tempted to squash Annabeth's ex like a bug.

"Ahhhh! Save me, please! You gotta save me!" Under the weight of Dane's paw, Roger's voice was just a whisper now.

"Dane," Bill said sternly. "Annabeth needs you. Let me take care of this guy, and you go to her."

Annabeth. Dane swayed, torn between his primal desire to rip Roger Pemberton into quivering chunks of bloody meat for what he'd done to Annabeth and his need to be at his injured mate's side.

"Dane? What do you mean, 'Dane?'" Roger demanded as Dane reluctantly released him.

Roger scrambled to his feet and staggered over to the sheriff.

"Shoot it! Shoot it now! Please!" he begged in a panicky tone. "It's a bear!"

Dane shifted smoothly back to human and saw Roger gape at him.

"I don't see a bear," he said to Bill. "Do you?"

Bill shook his head. "Just a big naked guy."

"What? What the fuck is going on here? How did you do that?" Roger's voice was shrill with panic.

As Roger continued to gape at Dane, obviously unable to believe what he'd just seen, Bill took the opportunity to cuff Roger's hands behind his back and read him his rights.

Once Roger had been shoved into the back seat of the sheriff's car, Bill popped the trunk and pulled out a pair of sweats.

"Now, put some clothes on before we head back into town," he said, tossing the sweats over to Dane. "Or I'll have to arrest you for public indecency."

18

BURNED

"This is going to sound really weird, but I thought I saw you turn into a bear last night," Annabeth said hoarsely when Dane showed up in her hospital room just as dawn was breaking.

She had spent the remaining hours of the night at Steele Memorial in Salmon, being treated for smoke inhalation. Her throat felt like it had been sandpapered, her chest hurt, her eyes were red and sore, and her mouth tasted foul.

And she felt very lucky that it hadn't been worse.

But whatever chemicals she'd been exposed to inside the burning had given her a doozy of a hallucination.

Instead of laughing, as she had expected, Dane looked stricken...and guilty.

He was still clad in the ill-fitting sweats he had been wearing when he returned to the bakery just as the other firefighters were putting out the last flames.

His face was covered with dark stubble, his hair was rumpled and sticking up at odd angles, and he looked exhausted. And sexy as hell.

"Uh, about that," he began. "I've been meaning to talk to you about some of the, uh, unique aspects of living in Bearpaw Ridge."

"What?" she asked, feeling confused.

Dane sighed. "It—well, it wasn't a hallucination. I—my entire family—we're bear shifters. I was trying to the find the right time to tell you."

"Bear shifters," she repeated, and a few of the odd things she'd noticed over the past few weeks fell into place. "Wait—*that* was your big secret? That's why you've got super-strength?"

He nodded, looking at the floor.

She blinked. Either she'd gone completely nuts, or the world had just turned upside down.

Bear shifters. Dane can turn into a bear.

It was unbelievable, but it made sense, too, in a weird way.

Something else occurred to her. "And Kayla? Is she a bear shifter, too? I caught her lifting my Hobart, and it weighs a lot more than she does!"

Dane nodded. "I'm sorry I didn't tell you sooner. I wanted to, but I just couldn't…"

His voice trailed off, and his face turned red. He wouldn't meet her eyes, just kept his gaze fixed firmly on the polished linoleum of the floor.

"But we're supposed to be getting married! Is that the kind of secret you'd keep from your wife?" Annabeth asked.

She didn't really feel angry at him…just really, really tired.

After everything that had happened yesterday and last night, after everything she had just lost, she didn't have the energy for anger. She was completely drained.

Her laptop, photo albums, and manila folder, still reeking of smoke, were stacked on the visitor's chair next to her bed. She still didn't know how much had been destroyed in the fire, but even if nothing else was left, Evan and Dane had managed to save the most important things.

"I'm sorry," Dane repeated. "It was wrong of me. I was just…scared."

Annabeth stared at him. Dane—big, strong Dane, who ran into burning buildings and could apparently turn himself into an eight-foot tall grizzly bear—had been *scared*?

"You're not from Bearpaw Ridge," he continued in an apologetic tone. "I was afraid you'd leave me if you found out that I wasn't entirely human."

"I may freak out about it later," she warned him. "Right now, I just feel numb. I'm exhausted, and I don't even know if I still have bed to sleep in...or a bakery."

"Let me take you home to the ranch," Dane said, meeting her gaze at last. His eyes were filled with deep compassion, and she knew then that the news wasn't good.

"You can stay at my place as long as you need to. Take a shower, get some sleep, eat something, then I'll drive you into town and we can look at your bakery and your apartment." He paused. "I'm so glad you're safe. When I realized that you were trapped in your loft..." He swallowed hard. "I love you, Annabeth. I don't know what I'd do if something happened to you."

"I love you, too." Bear shifter or not, that much was true.

She began to cough from all of the talking and reached for the glass of water by her bedside. As Dane watched her with a concerned expression, she sipped at it, trying to soothe her sore throat.

When she could speak again, she asked, "What happened?"

"There's going to be an arson investigation, but from what we can tell, Roger soaked the bakery and the stairs leading up to your apartment with gasoline before setting the place on fire. And he made sure that the on-call firefighters would be out of town, rushing to the scene of an imaginary car accident he called in before he began torching your place." Dane paused, his face and voice hard. "Bill Jacobsen arrested Roger last night as he was attempting to flee town. He's behind bars, facing charges of arson and attempted murder, among other things."

"Okay, good," Annabeth said. She was so tired that the room was beginning to revolve around her in slow circles. "I'll come home with you. But first…can I have a hug? I really need one right now."

Dane's arms, strong, comforting, and familiar, were around her before she finished speaking.

"It's going to be okay, Annabeth. No matter what happens, as long as we're together, it's going to be okay."

No, I don't think it's going to be okay, Annabeth thought later that afternoon as she stood on the sidewalk and gazed in shock at the gutted ruin of her bakery.

All the expensive plate glass windows were shattered, the brick façade was stained black with soot, and everything inside was blackened and melted into twisted lumps.

Dane put his arm around her shoulders. "You had insurance, right?" he asked quietly.

She nodded. "Yes, but I don't think it's going to be enough to replace all my equipment, fittings, and furnishings. A commercial bakery oven alone costs as much as a new car!"

And it gets worse.

She hesitated before continuing, "And I may not get anything at all. I talked to Jennifer before we drove out here—" Jennifer Jacobsen, the sheriff's daughter, was Annabeth's insurance agent, "and she told me that the insurance company won't pay the claim until they've finished an investigation. She warned me that there might be some issues with proving I had nothing to do with the arson, because Roger and I knew each other, and he's still insisting that he's my fiancé."

Dane growled and gave her a comforting squeeze.

"It'll be okay," he said, repeating what had become a mantra over the past few hours. "We'll find a way to make it okay."

Annabeth shook her head, unable to summon even the faintest spark of optimism. She still felt exhausted, even after a long nap, a shower, breakfast, and several cups of a soothing mint herb tea generously laced with honey.

Dane looked up at her loft. "I don't think it's going to take too much work to renovate your apartment. The fire never got up that far—except for your stairs, I'm betting it's mostly smoke and water damage."

Annabeth shuddered. Roger had targeted those stairs, intending to trap her inside the loft.

Even if she could afford to make the apartment livable again, she didn't ever want to spend another night there.

"Oh honey," Maggie said, later that afternoon, when Annabeth called her to tell her what had happened. "I'm so sorry, and I'm so glad you're okay! That's the most important thing, right?" She sighed into the phone. "I always knew that Roger was bad news. Thank God you weren't badly hurt or killed! I hope he rots in prison. And you're going to rebuild, right? Start over?"

"I want to," Annabeth said, fighting down the feeling of sick despair that had been growing since Dane had driven her into town and she'd seen the damage. "But I really can't do anything until I get the insurance payment. And even then…"

"And how's Dane treating you?" Maggie demanded. "Is he being supportive? If not, I'll head over and kick his ass!"

Annabeth laughed despite her black mood. "He's been great. In fact, I'm staying at his place for now." She looked around at the comfortable Edwardian interior of Dane's house, which was located about half a mile from the ranch's main house. "It's really nice. And he saved my life last night."

"Good!" Maggie said. "It's about time you found a man who appreciates you properly!"

"About that," Annabeth said, hesitantly. "You grew up in Bearpaw Springs, right?"

"Yep, hometown girl all the way," Maggie agreed. "Why? What's up?"

Okay, now's the part where I get to sound completely nuts.

Annabeth took a deep breath. "I saw Dane turn into a bear last night. He told me that most of the people who live around here can turn into animals. Am—am I crazy, Maggie?"

Maggie was silent for an uncomfortably long time.

"Hell of a way to find out," she said finally. "And you're not crazy, Annabeth. Or not crazier than anyone else living in that town." She laughed. "I'm a jaguar shifter myself. I love living in San Francisco, but it's hard sometimes, having to hide what I am all the time."

"You're a shapeshifter too?" In all the years they had known each other, Annabeth had never noticed anything odd about Maggie.

"And I'm still deep in the closet, honey, so don't you tell anyone in the City!" Maggie said, making Annabeth laugh again.

That set off another coughing fit and the need for more water.

When Annabeth had stopped coughing, Maggie said, "Anyhow, yes, Bearpaw Springs is a shifter settlement. There are a few of them, here and there, mostly in the middle of nowhere, for obvious reasons. Nearly all of the people living in and around the town are members of shifter families, though not all of them can actually shift into animals."

Annabeth felt her world shift a little further off-kilter at the revelation. "Oh, Maggie, what am I going to do now? I'm broke, and I'm not sure I should actually marry a guy who turns into a bear!"

"Why ever not? Dane Swanson is a hell of a nice guy, and you've been telling me that he's been a great boyfriend," Maggie said, sounding surprised.

"Well, he lied to me about being a shapeshifter, for one thing!" Annabeth said.

"Can you really blame him?" Maggie asked. "Look, it's one thing to grow up in Bearpaw Ridge, where even the non-shifters know about the shifter families living there. But to tell an outsider, *hey, I'm a shapeshifter, and my alter ego is a giant grizzly bear*...take it from me, honey, it's hard to out yourself to someone who doesn't believe that shifters even exist."

"I guess you're right," Annabeth said.

"Look, I've known Dane since we were kids," Maggie continued. "He's a good guy, and from everything you've told me, he's head over heels for you. Just give him the benefit of the doubt, okay? His secret...*our* secret...isn't an easy one to talk about."

19

REBORN

"Bethie, I don't understand why you don't just come home," her mother said, when Annabeth phoned her after dinner to tell her about the fire. "You've lost everything and you still have to pay off that loan. If you came home, you could move in with me, rent-free, and go to work for Maggie again at Cacao."

"I appreciate the offer, Mom, really I do," Annabeth said.

Out of the corner of her eyes, she saw Dane, sitting on the couch next her, stiffen in alarm. She reached over and patted his hand reassuringly.

"But you know I'm engaged to Dane. We're getting married the weekend after Labor Day, remember? I thought you were coming."

"Of course I'm coming, if you really want to go ahead with this wedding to a man *I've* never met, and who you *just* met," her mother said waspishly. "But I think you're making a big mistake, Annabeth."

"A bigger mistake than moving in with Roger?" Annabeth asked acidly. "I remember you were all for that."

A hurt silence on the line, and Annabeth instantly regretted her sharp words.

"Mom, I'm sorry. It's been a really stressful couple of days, and I'm on edge. Please come to the wedding. I know you'll love Dane and his family when you meet them."

"Oh, Bethie, you know I only want the best for you! And you almost burned to death!" Her mother sniffled, which made Annabeth feel even worse about what she'd said.

She ended the call quickly after that and found herself staring down at her phone.

Her thoughts returned to her dilemma—what *was* she going to do if the insurance payment didn't come through? How could she support herself?

As if reading her thoughts, Dane said, very quietly, "If you really want to return to California, I'll come with you."

Annabeth stared at him. He looked completely sincere.

"But the ranch—" she began. "Your home!"

"Mark can take over as ranch manager. He's a lawyer and better at the tax stuff than I am, anyway. I've got a business degree, so I'm sure I could find a job in the Bay Area."

"But—"

"My home is with you, wherever you are," he said firmly. "You're my mate, Annabeth. I can't live without you, not now."

She couldn't believe what she was hearing. Dane was willing to uproot himself, leave behind all of his friends and family and the firefighting job he loved…all for her?

Annabeth's eyes stung with tears. No one had ever done that for her. She had always been the one to compromise, to make sacrifices so that everything ran smoothly.

After her talk with Maggie, Annabeth was feeling better about the whole shapeshifter thing. And after some reflection, she realized Maggie was right. Dane's secret hadn't been an easy one for him to keep, and learning it hadn't changed the way that Annabeth felt about him.

"I don't want to leave Bearpaw Ridge," she told him. "But… thank you."

She put her phone on the table and climbed into his lap. Cradling his face in her hands, she kissed him thoroughly.

"I want you," he said, his fingers digging into her hips through the skirt he had bought her to replace the scrubs given to her by the hospital. "Oh, God, Annabeth, I almost lost you last night."

In reply, she leaned back just far enough to pull off the tank top she wore, followed by her bra.

Dane devoured her breasts, nipping and teasing her sensitive nipples with his tongue until she was squirming helplessly against him, desperate for relief from the heat he had kindled between her legs.

"Please, Dane," she moaned.

He put his hands under her buttocks and rose to his feet as if she weighed nothing. "You're not wearing panties, are you?"

She shook her head.

She could feel the bulge in his jeans pressing against her, and she wanted it badly. She wrapped her legs eagerly around his hips and rubbed herself against him.

"Good."

Dane pushed her against the nearest wall and reached down to unfasten his jeans with one hand.

"I'm going to fuck you now. I can see how ready you are for me," he said, his voice low, intense.

Liquid heat rushed through her at his words. She kissed him with frantic hunger and felt his hands slide under her thighs, lifting and spreading her wide for him.

Panting, she arched eagerly and felt the broad head of his cock nudge against her slick, swollen folds.

He thrust into her in a strong, smooth invasion, stretching her, filling her completely. Then, still pressing her against the wall, Dane pinned Annabeth's wrists over her head and kissed her throat.

"You feel so good," he said between kisses.

She moaned and tightened her legs around his hips.

He began to move, taking her hard and fast as she writhed against the wall, stretched taut in his grip.

As he thrust into her with powerful strokes, she felt a coil of anticipation tighten in her body, then burst with an explosion of pleasure that made her cry out and convulse helplessly in his grasp, her heels digging into the small of his back.

Dane growled, and his movements sped up as he neared his own climax. He stiffened against her with a loud cry, and his thrusts became short and sharp.

He gradually slowed his movements, milking the last few ripples of pleasure from her before loosening his hold on her wrists.

Panting, she clung to him, cradled in his strong arms, her face buried in his neck as he carried her to the couch.

"Everything okay?" he whispered, curling up around her, spooning her, his hand pressed against her tummy.

"Yeah," she said, lacing her fingers through his. "I think I needed that."

He chuckled. "I think we both did. I love you, Annabeth."

"Love you, too, Dane." Bear or man, it was the unvarnished truth.

She loved him. *All* of him.

He kissed the back of her neck, and they cuddled together in comfortable silence for a while.

Then, hesitantly, Dane said, "I know I should have told you about being a shifter. But I had a bad experience the last time I tried telling someone who didn't know about shifters, and I was afraid I was going to lose you."

"What happened?" Annabeth asked.

"I met someone in my final year at Colorado State…her name was Tanya," Dane began, and Annabeth remembered Kayla mentioning someone by that name. "I fell for her pretty hard. She'd grown up on a ranch in Texas, and I thought that she'd be the perfect wife for me—beautiful, brainy, close to getting her Agribusiness degree, and from a ranching family. I figured that she knew what she was getting into, marrying a rancher."

"As opposed to me, a clueless city girl whose biggest talent is baking cinnamon rolls," Annabeth said wryly.

"Don't undersell yourself, sweetheart," Dane said. "Your bakery was on its way to becoming a big success. You've got the three B's that drive me crazy: brains, beauty, and business sense."

Annabeth felt warmed by his respect. "So, Tanya?" she prompted.

Dane sighed. "Anyhow, we dated for a while, and things started to get serious. So, one evening, I told her about being a shifter. She was convinced I was either pulling her leg or crazy…so I showed her."

"Uh-oh," Annabeth said. She didn't like where this story was going, didn't like the tension she felt in Dane's body, pressed tightly against her.

"Yeah," Dane said. "My only excuse was that I was young and stupid. And I'd grown up in a shifter community. I was warned about keeping it a secret when I went away to college, but I didn't know what a…*shock* that finding out would be to ordinary humans."

"And Tanya freaked out?" Annabeth asked gently.

"I'd never seen anyone so scared. She ran out of the house we shared, jumped into her car, and drove away. I didn't follow her. I wanted to give her chance to calm down." Dane was silent for a long time, and she thought he had finished his story. Then he said, "I know now that I should have stopped her from driving when she was so upset and panicked. The police contacted me a couple of hours later and told me that she'd gotten into an accident. A bad one." Dane's arms tightened around Annabeth. "She didn't make it."

"Oh, Dane, I'm so sorry," Annabeth said, imagining the pain this must have caused him.

"So that's why I was so nervous about telling you about being a shifter. It's not easy to believe, and I didn't want you to leave me."

"I'm not going to leave you." Annabeth turned in his arms and kissed him, feeling an enormous surge of tenderness. "You make me happy, Dane. I don't want to move back to California. What I want to do is to stay in Bearpaw Ridge and marry you."

"Good," he breathed.

"And if the insurance payment doesn't come through, and it probably won't, I—I promise I'll start looking for a job as soon as I can. And maybe, some day, I'll be able to save up enough money to open another bakery."

"I have an idea that might help with that," Dane told her, gathering her against his chest. "Let me talk to a few people, and I'll let you know."

A month later, Annabeth found herself standing in front of a large crowd, a microphone in hand and Dane by her side, holding her free hand.

It was a beautiful June afternoon, and a huge feast had been set up in the meadow that ran down to the river.

The tall cottonwoods lining the riverbanks provided welcome shade, and picnic tables and benches had been set up under big canopies.

The air was filled with fragrant smoke and the delectable smells of cooking meat from the big barbecues set up by the owners of the Bear-B-Q Pit, who had donated huge slabs of seasoned pork ribs to accompany the Grizzly Creek Ranch's own steaks and brisket, while long tables groaned under the weight of side dishes—a variety of salads donated by the Brown Bear Market, pasta dishes from The Bear's Lair, vegetables, baked beans, cornbread, and other goodies brought by guests from neighboring ranches.

The Bearpaw Brewing Company had donated several kegs of their beer, and Dane's brothers had driven over a hundred miles to the nearest Costco and returned with the ranch's truck loaded to the gills with huge flats of soda and bottled water as well as napkins, paper plates, disposable cups, and giant bags of chips and gallons of salsa.

With Kayla and Elle's help and using the Grizzly Creek Ranch's big kitchen, Annabeth had made all the desserts for the event, baking a variety of cakes, pies, and tarts in addition to several hundred cookies, lemon bars, brownies, and, of course, her famous cinnamon rolls.

"I'd like to thank everyone for coming," she said shyly into the microphone, and the boisterous crowd quieted down immediately.

Looking around, she saw that there were at least 600 people in attendance and that she recognized most of them as having stopped by her bakery at least once or twice.

"I'm overwhelmed by your support and your generosity. Thank you so much for pulling my buns out of the fire."

She paused as a wave of laughter greeted her remark.

Holding a community fund-raiser BBQ and auction to help rebuild her bakery had been Dane's idea, but Elle had not only lent her whole-hearted support but had spread the word to her huge network of friends and acquaintances in the area.

"I want to thank my fiancé, Dane, and my future mother-in-law, Elle, for organizing this event. I'd also like to thank everyone who helped make today's event possible by donating food and auction items. You guys are amazing, and I'm humbled by the sense of community here."

She paused to wipe her eyes, which were welling over with tears of happiness.

"Last month, I stood in front of the smoking ruins of my bakery, thinking that I had lost everything and that I was finished. In my shock and grief, I didn't realize how much I still had—my new family, my friends, and everyone in Bearpaw Ridge. Today, you've given me the hope of a new start, and I can't tell you how much that means to me. Thank you, everyone, and thank you for making me feel at home here. I love you all!"

"But especially me, I hope," Dane joked, and gave her a quick kiss to the sound of whoops and applause.

"And with that," he said, taking the microphone from her, "we'll start the auction. First up, a Shakespeare Ugly Stik GX2

6.5 foot Medium Heavy rod with a Penn Battle II 5000 spinning reel, donated by the Bearpaw Fish n' Game Store. Starting bid is $75—that's half of the retail price. Do I hear 75?"

The bidding on the first item was lively. And there were lots of other items to go, all of them donated by individuals and businesses in Bearpaw Ridge.

Annabeth had donated two items: a gift certificate for a wedding or special occasion cake for up to 500 servings, and her sapphire pendant, cleaned and polished after it was recovered from her loft.

The hottest auction item was an all-inclusive fall weekend getaway for two at the nearby Bearpaw Springs Resort, with accommodation, hot springs admission, spa treatments, and dinner in the resort's restaurant, thanks to Manny Ornelas, who had managed to contact the resort's reclusive owner and ask for a donation.

As the auction continued during dinner, with Mark taking over the role of auctioneer so that she and Dane could grab something to eat, Annabeth saw her insurance agent Jennifer Jacobsen waving at her.

Bracing herself for bad news, she excused herself from the table with a promise to return to her half-eaten dinner. Dane immediately rose to follow her.

"Hey Annabeth, hi Dane, sorry to interrupt, but I really need to talk to Annabeth, and her phone was turned off." Jennifer looked around the milling crowd and the auction. "Though you probably wouldn't have been able to hear it ringing, anyway."

She turned back to Annabeth, who was clutching Dane's hand for comfort.

"I wanted to let you know that I just heard back from your insurance company, and after concluding their investigation, they've agreed that you had nothing to do with setting the fire. So they're going to pay your claim. I couldn't wait to tell you!"

Annabeth's knees went weak at the unexpected good news.

"Oh," she said stunned. "That's wonderful!"

She had filed a claim that included a long, painfully itemized list of everything she had lost in the fire, but she had lost hope of having her claim paid once the arson investigation began.

"I know!" Jennifer said. "Everyone in town was crossing their fingers for you! We all miss stopping by your place for breakfast treats. Does this mean you're going to reopen soon?"

"Yes!" said Annabeth. She looked up at Dane and smiled at him with heartfelt joy. "Oh, yes. As soon as possible."

EPILOGUE

"I do," said Annabeth, as she and Dane stood in front of the minister three-and-half months later.

The minister, who was also Dane's aunt Margaret, smiled. "I now declare you husband and wife. You may kiss."

The assembled group of 600 guests applauded as Dane kissed Annabeth with great enthusiasm.

When the kiss ended, leaving her weak-kneed, Annabeth saw her mother, seated in the front row next to Maggie Ornelas. Both of them were wiping their eyes and smiling. Mom looked beautiful in her cobalt-blue dress and pearls, and Maggie was wearing a dress with a bold floral print.

Maggie, grinning broadly, gave Annabeth a thumbs-up.

Their original plans for a small family wedding had burgeoned into a huge outdoor celebration, held in the same riverside meadow where the big fundraiser had been held at the beginning of the summer.

In a fit of expansiveness, Dane and Annabeth had concluded the auction that evening by inviting everyone present at the fundraiser to come to their wedding.

And most of them had.

It had been a busy summer of rebuilding and renovation, but Annabeth was able to reopen Cinnamon + Sugar just before Labor Day Weekend.

The interior had been completely redone to look like a classic European café with retro black-and-white floor tiles, Art Deco posters, and new bakery cases, tables, and chairs at the front. She had even found a couple of matching comfy leather armchairs at an estate sale and put them in one corner of the café.

Fred Barker and his sons had redone the building's wiring, as promised, and Annabeth had gone bargain-hunting on the Internet for reliable used commercial appliances, including an even bigger oven and a 60-quart Hobart floor mixer to replace the 40-quart mixer destroyed in the fire.

Thanks to the fund-raiser and auction, she was also able to repair the smoke and water damage to the loft above the bakery. She had rented it to a young shifter couple who had just moved to Bearpaw Ridge.

Annabeth had settled in nicely to Dane's house at the ranch and decided she really wouldn't mind getting up twenty minutes earlier to drive into town to start work.

In July, using the big kitchen at the Grizzly Creek Ranch's main house while the bakery renovation was still a work-in-progress, she had baked and decorated the cake she had promised Fred and Linda Barker for their daughter's wedding.

She had delivered it in her trusty Prius and had assembled the tiers on-site at the Bearpaw Springs Resort's restaurant.

In an unexpected bonus, the restaurant manager had contacted Annabeth immediately after the wedding and asked if she'd be interested in becoming one of the resort's preferred wedding vendors.

Annabeth had enthusiastically agreed, and Dane's youngest brother Ashton had promptly created a website for her new Special Occasion Cakes service.

Within two weeks, Annabeth had found herself with more wedding cake orders than she could handle for the rest of summer, and she actually had to turn away business, even with Kayla's help.

Elle had graciously ceded control of the big kitchen, with its generous counter space, to Annabeth's new mixers, pans, and cake decorating equipment, all hastily purchased at the restaurant supply warehouse to replace the items ruined in the fire.

Kayla cheerfully switched roles from barista to baking assistant and delivery driver. Her shifter strength meant that she was a huge help in delivering the large, heavy, tiered wedding cakes.

The stream of orders had meant that Annabeth was able to continue making her mortgage payments on the bakery building throughout the summer and also pay for upgraded appliances.

Annabeth knew she'd miss Kayla when her assistant departed to start veterinary school in the fall, but Kayla had already mentioned that her sister was interested in coming to work at the bakery.

"See, I told you everything was going to turn out okay," Dane whispered as they looked out over the sea of faces gathered to witness their marriage.

He was right.

Standing in front of her assembled family, friends, and neighbors on a beautiful autumn afternoon, with Dane at her side, Annabeth Jones Swanson realized that she had found her happily ever after.

The End

Thank you so much for reading my story. The series continues in Book 2, *Smolder!*

The last thing that Mark Swanson expects is for an accident victim to be his fated mate… especially when she turns out to be the reporter behind the news site determined to expose shifters as real. Despite the risks, Mark and his bear can't resist getting closer to the sexy reporter they both want to claim. The heat between them is irresistible—but when a shifter hit man shows up, it's clear that Caitlyn's got more problems than a wrecked car. Find out what happens in *Smolder!*

For news about upcoming releases and special promotions, please sign up for my email list at http://eepurl.com/b0ojU1 or find me on Facebook at http://www.facebook.com/OpheliaSextonAuthor.

Want a free sneak peek at my upcoming books before they're published? I'm always looking for Advance Review Team members! If you're willing to read prepublication editions of my books and leave a review on Amazon when the book is published, sign up here: http://eepurl.com/b9iiaT

I am currently hard at work on the next Bearpaw Ridge Firefighters book.

BOOKS BY OPHELIA SEXTON

Bearpaw Ridge Firefighters

- *Heat (Bearpaw Ridge Firefighters Book 1)*
- *Smolder (Bearpaw Ridge Firefighters Book 2)*
- *Ignite (Bearpaw Ridge Firefighters Book 3)*
- *Flame (Bearpaw Ridge Firefighters Book 4)*
- *Burn (Bearpaw Ridge Firefighters Book 5)*
- *Ash (Bearpaw Ridge Firefighters Book 6)*
- *Smoke (Bearpaw Ridge Firefighters Book 7)*
- *Blaze (Bearpaw Ridge Firefighters Book 8)*
- *Ember (Bearpaw Ridge Firefighters Book 9)*
- *Christmas in July (A Bearpaw Ridge Firefighters novella)*
- *Inferno (Bearpaw Ridge Firefighters Book 10)*
- *Scorch (Bearpaw Ridge Firefighters Book 11)*

Rocky Mountain Smokejumpers

- *Hard Landing (Rocky Mountain Smokejumpers Book 1)*
- *Jump Point (Rocky Mountain Smokejumpers Book 2)*

Beast Warriors (co-authored with Bliss Devlin)

- *Fugitive: A Werebear + BBW Paranormal Romance (Beast Warriors Book 1)* by Bliss Devlin and Ophelia Sexton
- *Hunter: A Werebear + BBW Paranormal Romance (Beast

Warriors Book 2) by Bliss Devlin and Ophelia Sexton
- *Leader: A Werebear + Dragon Shifter Paranormal Romance (Beast Warriors Book 3)* – coming soon!

Made in United States
Orlando, FL
10 February 2025